Keep
your hair
on !

Elizabeth Vercoe is an Australian artist and mother of three young children, who is based in Melbourne. *Keep Your Hair On!* is her first book and results from her experience of having cancer at a young age.

Elizabeth says: 'When I was little I dreamed of being all sorts of things. An air hostess, a truck driver, an actor, a circus clown, a journalist, a pilot, a tree planter, a park ranger. Then, when I was older, twenty-five years old, I got cancer.

'This was the beginning of an amazing journey. I saw some very dark and bleak times. I was frightened of living this way. But mostly I was terrified of dying.

'When I was at the lowest and darkest point of my journey, I made a discovery: there is light even in darkness. Six simple words.

'It is almost ten years since my dalliance with cancer. I don't like calling it a battle because I was not really at war with myself. *Keep Your Hair On!* has been sitting inside me for a long time.'

Keep your hair on!

Elizabeth Vercoe

Piccadilly Press • London

First published in Australia in 2003 by Black Dog Books.
This revised edition first published in the UK in 2004
by Piccadilly Press Ltd.,
5 Castle Road, London, NW1 8PR
www.piccadillypress.co.uk

A catalogue record for this book is available
from the British Library

ISBN: 185340 885 9 (trade paperback)

1 3 5 7 9 10 8 6 4 2

Printed and bound in Great Britain by Bookmarque Ltd
Text design by Textype
Cover illustration by Sue Hellard. Cover design by Fielding Design
Set in Goudy

For Fabio, Jacob, Luca and Tahli –
and all their hair

Chapter 1

Down the Plughole

Jess watched as her hair went down the plughole. Damn. It was really happening.

Thoughts of her life flashed past. Jess was sixteen and had never had a serious boyfriend. Until now. She'd kissed two boys in her whole life – one on the beach at Lorne, who didn't really count. She hadn't spoken to him afterwards. The other boy counted a lot. So far, they'd gone out together six times. Dylan was almost as shy as Jess, so it was huge for him to tell her that he really liked her (more than anyone else he'd ever liked). Which he had done. About two weeks ago, at the bus stop. And then, they'd had their far-and-away best-ever kiss (not in front of anyone though).

She'd never wagged school. She had smoked half a packet of cigarettes one night in the car park of the shopping centre. Waste of money. She had almost spewed and she'd coughed for four days. Chunky bits and all. She played the piano and was on a mixed netball team. Her position was centre and occasionally wing attack.

Her best friends at school were Charlotte and Sara. Charlotte had a boyfriend, Joffa, who drove a hotted-up V8 Commodore. Too fast, mostly. Jess liked hanging around with Charlotte. There was something cool about the way her jumper always smelled of stale cigarette smoke. Most other kids were scared of her. Charlotte was hip and she was smart.

Sara didn't smoke but she had eaten three cigarettes once for a dare. And she was funny. You'd nearly wet your pants from laughing when Sara was on a roll.

Damn. The water was getting clogged in the shower base. Jess bent down to retrieve the hair – it was matted and there was enough to fill her clenched fist. Even more had made it down the drain.

'Jess, are you all right in there?'

Funny how mothers were always around, even when you didn't want them to be. Friends were more inconsistent. They couldn't be there all the time and often they didn't know what to say.

'Yep.' Jess put on her best 'I'm all right' voice, which was halfway between a sob and a groan but actually sounded a bit like a strangled cat. 'I'll be out soon.'

'OK – don't use all the hot water.'

Jess absent-mindedly ran her fingers under the lukewarm shower spray, which was getting colder by the second. She turned the taps off.

People had been great so far. It had been hard getting over the shock – it's not every day that you're told you have cancer – but life seemed to be slowly getting back to normal. They'd told Jess she had lymphatic cancer, which would possibly be cured using chemotherapy, once a month, over six months.

She had been through her first treatment. Which was why she felt like crap. And why her hair was falling out. It had been thinning for three days, but today every last strand was coming out. In big

3

clumps. Jess wiped the steam off the mirror and looked at her face. She tried not to let her gaze wander to the top of her head but kept her focus on her eyes. Greeny brown. More green in the centre. Pupils big and black. White bits red. Now she noticed that she was crying. Silent tears – collecting in the corners of her eyes. Inside she felt nothing. Her anger had gone and there was a numb, almost cold, feeling.

She leaned over and threw up into the toilet. She was beginning to understand the advantages of having the loo in the bathroom. There was a knot in the pit of her stomach. Carefully and slowly she rinsed her mouth out and cleaned her teeth. The chemo made her spew and left huge ulcers in her mouth – 'immuno-suppression' the doctors called it.

She bent over to wrap a towel around her hair and a cold draught ran up the nape of her neck, over the back of her skull. She lifted her head slowly.

Damn. Already she'd forgotten. She reached into the bottom of the bathroom bin and fished out the matted clumps of hair that she'd just thrown away. She felt kind of embarrassed and didn't want anyone else to see them. They wouldn't flush away – just

4

floated at the top of the toilet bowl. So she hooked them out with her hairbrush, dumped the lot back in the bin and tied a knot in the top of the plastic liner. Then she covered her head with her towel – turban style – and looked in the mirror again.

This was the hardest thing Jess had ever been through. Her mind raced. A fleeting grin crossed her face as she imagined Charlotte and Sara shaving their heads in sympathy with her. Charlotte would want to stand out, though. She'd shave her head, then get a Mohawk wig straight away – she was always threatening her dad that she'd run away and become a punk – and Sara would stain her head black and pretend to be a bowling ball or something. Jess snorted. A laugh and a cry at the same time. Her legs went weak so she sat on the edge of the bath.

Jess had never felt more alone in her life. It wasn't so much because her hair had fallen out – although that was certainly part of it – but because even if her friends *did* shave their heads there would still be a huge gap between them.

A canyon.

An abyss.

The worst bit was keeping it secret. Her teachers

knew, and she'd told Charlotte and Sara (who were sworn to secrecy, just as her family was). But not Dylan. It was so hard not telling him. Luckily, he worked, so he didn't see her every day at school. A couple of the others in her class seemed to know – sometimes she could feel silent stares. But if they knew, they weren't saying anything. At least, not to Jess's face.

One of her classmate's brothers – a Year Seven kid – had even asked her if she was contagious. Jess couldn't believe it. Charlotte straight away had offered to mash his face into the drinking taps but Jess just said, 'No, I'm not cont-t-t-agious,' and rolled her eyes and frothed at the mouth. The kid ran away.

Charlotte had laughed so much that Pepsi had come out her nose. Just quietly, Jess had admired the boy's courage. It was much better than the silent stares others gave her. She felt a bit guilty about scaring him – she'd apologise when she saw him again.

'Jess – get out. I'll be late.'

Spud was her twelve-year-old brother. He never had a shower in the morning but always had to stick

6

his tufty hair down. He was an all right kid.

'One more minute.'

Jess splashed cold water on to her face and carefully applied black mascara. She pulled a woolly hat out of the bottom drawer of the bathroom cabinet. She had bought it last week, the day before she'd kissed Dylan. Secretly she had hoped – in her heart – that she wouldn't have to use it. The towel fell to the floor as Jess pulled the woolly hat over her scalp. Lucky it was cold today.

Slowly and deliberately, Jess hung her towel on the rail. She took a deep breath and opened the bathroom door. The air in the passage was cold but Jess's heart and eyes were blazing as she prepared to face the day.

Chapter 2

Bald as a Slimy Toad

Twenty past eight. As usual, the school bus was running late. It's nice to know some things don't change, thought Jess as she stood in the freezing cold air, rubbing her hands to keep warm.

There was steam curling about her head from the moisture on her breath. In the distance, Sara was walking with some other kids and pretending she had a real smoke in her hand. She could almost blow smoke rings with her breath! Their happy voices drew closer. Jess pulled her woolly hat down a bit and tucked her scarf into the top of her jumper. Thank goodness she could wear her tracksuit pants and a thick woollen jumper to school. There were no uniforms for the senior kids at Benfield High. She would have felt really self-conscious about her stick insect skinny legs if she'd had to wear the stupid skirt and tights that had been compulsory up until last year.

'Hey, Jess.' Sara had finished air smoking and was almost at the bus stop. 'Nice hat.'

Jess half smiled. She cringed a bit too. The woolly-hat comments would be sure to come thick and fast all day. Although the majority of her hair had fallen out completely, there were still a few wispy strands left. She wasn't quite ready to share her new look with the rest of the world. Not yet.

A thought occurred to Jess. 'Sara, have you got your nail scissors with you?' she asked.

'Yep.' Sara never went anywhere without her little 'survival kit' containing scissors, a mirror, safety pins, needles and dental floss. No one – including Sara – quite knew why, but it meant she was always handy to have around. 'Here you are.'

She handed Jess the scissors – pointy end first – with a little pretend stab as though she was jousting.

'Hang on, I'll need you to help me. Over here.' Jess motioned Sara over to the big fat gum tree that was at least a hundred years old and wide enough for the two of them to hide behind. This was where Dylan had first told Jess he was falling for her in a big way. And where they'd had that amazing kiss. Had it really been just two weeks ago? The tree probably kept all sorts of secrets in its sturdy branches.

'Jess, if you think you're gonna drag me around behind that tree the way you did with Dylan . . .' Sara was sniggering and amusing herself greatly.

'Oh, shut up and come over here.'

'Just be gentle with me . . .' Sara trembled with mock fear and then skipped over.

Safely behind the tree, Jess took her woolly hat off. 'Look, I'm as bald as a badger.'

Sara took a deep breath. It took her a moment to compose herself. Then, trying to contain her surprise, and with her usual style, she said, 'Don't be stupid. Badgers aren't bald. *Frogs* are bald. *Toads* are bald. You're bald as a slimy toad.'

'Thanks a lot.' Jess was trying to be casual but she didn't feel very convincing.

'Hey, don't worry.' Sara's tone was gentler now, more comforting. 'It looks good. It actually suits you. You never know, you might start a trend. The Jess McAllister look, available at your hairdresser now.'

'Yeah, right,' Jess said. But she felt a bit better.

'My mum would say, "Well, at least you've got the right shaped head for it!" I'm not kidding, Jess. It looks fantastic – it does really suit you.'

'Thanks. Anyway, I wanted you to cut these wispy bits off before we get to school.' Jess turned around to show Sara the 'tails' that were growing from the base of her neck.

'Are you kidding? Jeez, some kids would kill to have tails like those and you want to cut them off.'

'Sara – '

'Yeah, yeah. I'm just kidding around. I think it would look cooler without them too. Come here.'

With a few snips, the job was done.

'So, when did it happen?' asked Sara quietly.

'This morning, in the shower.'

'Did you feel it – like, did it hurt or anything?'

'Nah. It just came out in handfuls as I was washing it. Pretty freaky.'

'Mmmm.'

There was a silence.

'I'll be OK. It just stinks, this whole thing. And my ears are freezing.'

'Put your woolly hat back on.' Sara was packing

11

away her scissors. 'Come on, the bus is here.'

Jess pulled her woolly hat back over her ears and both girls ran towards the bus. The doors had closed, but the driver opened them again for Sara and Jess.

They stood in the stairwell. It was too crowded to even attempt moving further down. The windows were fogged up – too many people breathing – and covered with kids' finger-paintings. Luckily, the windscreen was clear. The driver leaned over to open the top sliding window above Jess and Sara.

'Yo, Spud,' called Sara at the top of her voice as Jess's little brother went hurtling by on his bike.

Spud barely glanced up. He gave them a quick wave and was gone. Spud was very light, and a mean machine when it came to speed and bikes. He liked to race the bus to school. So far, he'd beaten it every time.

It was a morning of spotting familiar faces from the bus window. And then there were another two. Dylan was on his way to work at the garage – his friend, Mike, was not far behind.

'Hey, there's Dylan.'

Jess had barely spoken the words before loudmouth Sara was screeching, 'Dylan!'

12

He looked over.

Jess smiled. Dylan smiled and waved. Mike looked up and nodded in their direction. Taking his cue from Dylan, he gave an uncomfortable wave too, and then shoved his hand deep into his pocket.

'Hey, Dylan, what do you think of Jess's new hairdo?' And before Jess knew what was happening, Sara had ripped her woolly hat off.

In that moment Jess could have killed Sara. She didn't know whether to laugh or to cry. Unable to speak, unable to move, Jess just stared at Dylan.

He would hate it, she was convinced. He would drop her like a sack of potatoes. He would never want to talk to her again. He would cross the street to avoid her. He and his mates would laugh and tell stories about the bald, slimy toad he had once hung out with.

Jess was mortified. All of this was churning about in her head for what seemed like an eternity. Time stopped. Still Jess stared at Dylan.

Then he smiled. Straight at her. He flicked that gorgeous lock of hair away from his eyes and called out, 'It looks great. Cool. I'll catch you after school.'

Jess was dumbfounded. She just nodded, as she pulled her hat back on.

The bus was finally driving away. In a state of utter disbelief, she waved to Dylan and half turned back to Sara. The bus hit a rock, causing the girls to bump into each other. Jolted back to reality with a thud, Jess belted Sara with her bag. Still uncertain as to whether she wanted to laugh or cry, Jess hissed, 'Don't you ever do anything like that again.'

'Like what?'

'You know exactly what. If you ever pull my woolly hat off again, I'll . . . I'll . . .'

'All right, I get the message. Keep your hair on.' Sara was grinning. Jess couldn't help herself – she smiled too.

The brief moment of tension was broken and both girls burst into giggles.

As usual, Charlotte was waiting for them at the school gate, jabbering away on her mobile. Jess had no idea how Charlotte paid her phone bills – when she wasn't talking she was texting. Charlotte could carry on a real-life conversation at the same time as she was furiously, two-handedly text-messaging someone else. If only the keyboard teacher could see how ambidextrous she really was!

Joffa stood leaning on the bonnet of his car with

14

his arms crossed and cigarettes tucked into the outside arm of his tight black T-shirt. To the untrained eye he looked a bit scary, but Charlotte seemed to have him wrapped round her little finger.

As the bus pulled up, Joffa slid into the driver's seat of his car and revved the engine. As if on cue, Charlotte shoved the phone into her pocket – she never used a school bag – and jumped off the bonnet. Joffa did a burn-out and, with a squeal of tyres and a blast from his musical horn, he sped off.

Charlotte stubbed out her smoke with a non-regulation Doc Marten boot and held out a packet to Jess.

'Chewy?' Her jaws were forever on the move. And then she noticed Jess's woolly hat, minus the dark, fuzzy hair that should have been poking out from underneath it.

'Jeez, mate, it finally happened then?'

'Yep. You now officially hang out with a skinhead.'

Jess thought that at least Charlotte would have some sort of clever comeback to that. But she said nothing. Instead, she was sort of quiet. Unusual for such a jabberjaw. Every report card she'd ever received had said, 'Charlotte should learn to listen more. Charlotte talks too much.'

'I reckon it's really cool.' Trust Sara to give Charlotte such a blatant cue.

'Are you OK?' Charlotte seemed unusually thoughtful.

Jess was a bit unnerved by how serious Charlotte had suddenly become.

'Yep, I'll cope,' Jess said brightly. She took a bit of gum. So did Sara. The school bell was just ringing and some of the younger kids were making a run for their classes.

'Sure you don't want to take up smoking? What's the worst that can happen – you'll get cancer and go bald!'

Hallelujah! The real Charlotte had not been abducted by aliens. She was back. And in fine form.

'Shut up, Charlotte.' Jess gave her a friendly punch and linked arms with both of her friends.

The three of them walked together up the path.

Chapter 3

Sick Bay

'I guess you'd better call my mum.' Jess was sitting on the cool tiles of the bathroom floor in the school's sick bay, in close communion with the toilet bowl.

She was feverish – her body wouldn't stop shaking and she was sweating profusely. She had just thrown up for the second time. Jess felt about as glamorous as a slimy toad.

'I've already called your mother; she's on her way. Just rest now.' Mrs Watson smiled down at Jess with large, sympathetic eyes and then crept through the door, closing it gingerly behind her.

They were getting to know one another quite well here in the sick bay, the nurse and the cancer patient. Jess had a tendency to push herself to the limit and was well known for her tenacity – she was fiercely independent and didn't want to be treated as though she were different. But some things, though, were just unavoidable. Puking, for instance.

'Just rest now.'

For a second Jess had felt like laughing in Mrs Watson's face. What on earth did she think Jess would do? Get up and do a tap dance or start building a block of flats? Jess hardly had the energy to laugh or even to hold her head up, let alone partake in an unrestful activity. Besides, her head was throbbing. It was taking all her strength to remain conscious.

At least she'd made it to lunchtime today. The past two days, she'd gone home straight after assembly. It wasn't that she loved school. But when she was at school, at least she could pretend that nothing was wrong.

Her mother had arrived. She could hear the sound of Ruby's strappy sandals clomping their way up the corridor. It was like being in an echo chamber inside the sick bay – which was especially awful if anyone else in there had a stomach bug. Lucky she wasn't trying to sleep.

The footsteps stopped. That meant her mother was talking to the woman at the reception desk. Soon she would clomp her way up the passage to Room Three, where Jess was. She would knock twice and say, 'I'm here, sweet pea,' and then the door would open, and, with a waft of sickly smelling perfume, there she'd be.

Ruby was a nurse and worked shifts at Benfield Private Hospital. She'd been taking time off to look after Jess, especially around the days when she had her chemotherapy. Ruby looked young for her age, and strangers often mistook Jess and her mother for sisters. Mostly, Jess was very grateful for all that her mother was doing for her. But sometimes it got on her nerves that she was being treated like a little kid again, and she knew that Spud sometimes got pissed off that he wasn't getting extra presents and ice creams and stuff as she was. But it was nothing that they couldn't handle. Yet.

Jess hadn't told her mum how much she felt for Dylan. She would have liked to and probably would have if she hadn't been sick. But now Ruby was becoming more and more protective. Something inside Jess was starting to rebel a bit, and she needed to keep certain aspects of her life to herself. She had so little control over what was being done to her body – sometimes it was like she wasn't a real person at all, just a lump of meat – that she needed to keep some things private.

Besides that, her mother would be sure to interfere. It would seem innocent enough. Ruby would just want to meet Dylan at the beginning. Then she would have to invite him round, when he would discover that Jess was sick. Her mother was a motor-mouth. She wouldn't be able to help herself. In fact, Jess's illness had become one of the main topics of conversation at home. It was a relief to have times when Jess could just act as if she were normal. Any second now . . .

There was a knock at the door. 'I'm here, sweet pea.'

There – Ruby's freshly made-up face and coiffed hair had appeared round the doorway, with the overwhelming barrage of perfume following closely behind.

'Your special cushion is in the car – do you think you can walk to the car park by yourself?'

Jess was pretty thankful that there was no one else

in sick bay to hear the 'sweet pea and special cushion' thing. 'Yep. I'll be all right as long as I can lean on you for balance.'

'Have you got your bag? Is there anything you need from your locker?' Before Jess could answer either question, her mother continued, 'Oh my God, you're so pale. You look awful.'

'Thanks.' Jess never knew what to say when Ruby carried on. Sarcasm was her standard coping strategy, but it was hard for her to speak. She needed to conserve her energy for the walk to the car.

Jess had almost mastered the art of making the complicated manoeuvre from sick bay to car park look effortless. She was like a swan gliding along the river. Looking all graceful on the surface but paddling like mad underneath. She just hoped that she wouldn't need to throw up on the way.

She made it. This time. Yesterday she hadn't been so fortunate. There was nothing more embarrassing than having a huge chunder in front of an audience. Nothing.

When she walked into the lounge room, Jess was surprised to see Spud sitting on the couch watching

21

television. Surprised and annoyed. One of the consolations of coming home early was catching up on the daytime soaps. Which you couldn't do, of course, when your spiky little brother was already sitting on the remote control.

'What are you doing at home, slackbum? Does Mum know you're here?' Jess asked. She was feeling a little chirpier now.

Spud just sort of shrugged and didn't look up. 'I'm sick.'

'What's wrong with you – social-studies-itis?' Jess chuckled in spite of her headache.

'Stomach ache and sore head if you must know.' Spud *was* looking a bit peaky. 'What's wrong with you today?'

'Cancer,' said Jess playfully, giving Spud's hair a bit of a ruffle as she walked behind the couch. She could make jokes now and then about her illness. Just now and then, when she was feeling OK.

Jess walked through to the kitchen and dumped her school bag. She opened the fridge door and just stood there for a while, looking. There was nothing inside that didn't make her feel like puking. She grabbed the last bit of flat ginger ale and swigged it out of the bottle. The ginger was meant to be good for soothing the stomach. So they told her, anyway. She had it when she was going in for chemo. That, and slippery elm powder in a yoghurt smoothie. Slippery elm was brilliant. It lined her stomach, it was natural, and it really helped to stop nausea.

Some bozo on television was screeching at his wife who was squealing back at him while the whole audience thundered and ranted at both of them. Riveting stuff. Jess headed for the sanctuary of her bedroom.

'Jess, do you want me to make you a salad sandwich?'

Ruby was always trying to make Jess eat salad sandwiches. She said it was because she was concerned that Jess had lost so much weight, but Jess was convinced that there was some sort of conspiracy afoot between her mother and the greengrocer. Surely there was some law against the amount of fresh food that her mother brought home? It seemed that every day her mother would drag Jess along to weird and wonderful health-care practitioners in the hope of finding a cure. It had started with a visit to a naturopath and continued with an iridologist and kinesiologist. Ruby had been gathering truckloads of information from a clinic that offered access to alternative treatments for illness. Funny, with her being a medical nurse and everything. Ruby was embracing the challenge, she said, and looking at all the options. Sometimes Jess wished that her mum would just stop. That she would hang out and listen to her and stuff, instead of rushing about everywhere.

Jess didn't feel like eating. 'No, thanks, Mum. I still feel sick.'

'Are you sure?'

Did Ruby think that Jess was a moron? That she couldn't make her own decision as to whether or not she felt like eating?

'Yes, I'm sure. I'm not hungry.'

'I've just got some lovely fresh tomatoes from the greengrocers. They're so juicy.'

'No.' Jess clenched her teeth. 'Thanks.'

'Well, if you're sure I can't tempt you . . .'

Jess slammed her bedroom door shut and tried to block out the rest of the world. Immediately, her thoughts turned to Dylan. Damn it! He had been going to meet up with her after school today. Jess sighed. Things just didn't seem to be going right. She really hoped that Sara had managed to find him and tell him that Jess had gone home early. Damn it. Jess kicked the rubbish bin. And stubbed her toe.

Chapter 4

What's Normal, Anyway?

Jess closed her eyes and slumped back on to her pillow. There seemed to be no escape. She took a few deep breaths. Sometimes slow breathing helped when she felt rotten like this.

Her toe was throbbing. After a moment she began to feel a little better. She was trying to remember how they taught her to relax when she went to yoga. Her forehead was wrinkled, and the area behind her eyes felt tired and stressed. Systematically, Jess worked her way down her entire body, trying to identify the parts that were tense.

Relax. Relax. Jess was mimicking the oh-so-soothing voice of the yoga teacher. She giggled a bit. It was working, though. She was beginning to feel better and her headache was lifting.

As she nestled into her bed, her mind wandered back over the events of the day. Although she had been seriously pissed off with Sara for ripping her hat off, in a funny kind of way she was glad too. There was an element of relief that her baldness was out in the open. And Dylan had seemed to like her bald head.

At first she had wanted to tell him about the big C and was all set to do it. But she never seemed able to find the right words, or the right time. There were some things it was really hard to talk about with a new boyfriend, and this was one of them. 'Oh, by the way, I've got cancer and I'm soon going to be bald and sick and I might die and I'll probably be really depressed – but hey, can we still go to the movies tonight?' She wasn't sure how he'd react. Sympathy was really hard to handle. Especially if it came from someone she liked as much as Dylan.

From an outside point of view, it may have seemed selfish of Jess not to tell Dylan about her illness. But all that Jess wanted was for Dylan to treat her as though she were normal. She wanted them to go rollerblading and go to movies and eat fish and chips in the park – all that crappy, fun, normal stuff. She didn't want the other distractions – the reality of her day-to-day life with cancer – to become the focus when she was with Dylan.

Hospital visits and treatments took for ever, and they seemed to suck the energy right out of her. Sometimes, she felt like she'd just been hit by a truck. On top of all this, her mind was constantly churning over things like dying and maybe not being able to have children because of the treatment. It sucked. None of it was fair. Plus, now all her hair had fallen out. Her eyelashes and eyebrows would be next. Along with the unmentionables. All of it. More and more, Jess was feeling like an alien or a circus freak.

And as time went by, it just seemed easier not to tell Dylan. So she hadn't.

Chapter 5

Secrets

Two weeks, three days, five hours and twenty-four minutes – Jess studied the second hand of her bedside clock for a moment – and twenty-eight seconds since Dylan had told Jess how strongly he felt about her. And since that to-die-for kiss, Jess couldn't stop thinking about him. She had seen him half a dozen times since then, including the time at the bus stop with Sara, and they had spoken twice on the phone.

Jess wondered if obsession was hereditary. Her mother had been known to carry on for hours – sometimes even whole days – about an ugly pair of chunky neck-breaking sandals or a disgustingly bright lurex top. Sometimes, Ruby's fashion sense left a lot to be desired. Dad used to joke, half seriously, that Ruby was obsessive–compulsive. 'She's a beautiful woman, your mother, but by God can she carry on like a pork chop about nothing.'

This memory took Jess by surprise. It wasn't often that she remembered moments of happiness or genuine affection between her parents. Dad lived in Queensland now. He had called when he found out Jess was sick, but she'd heard nothing since. Not that she was expecting much. Jess certainly didn't hold any illusions that her father would just turn up on the doorstep one day, although she'd be rapt if he did.

Jess felt a pang in her chest. Spud had all but stopped talking about the holiday of a lifetime Dad had taken them on five years before. They had been whisked off to Disneyland for a week. It had been so wonderful. So exciting. And they hadn't heard from their father since. Spud was trying so hard to pretend that he didn't care, but she knew he missed Dad. They both did. But she also knew that having both her parents in the same house was a nightmare. They just could not live together under the one roof. End of story. Jess hoped that she wouldn't turn out like that. And that her stupid cancer wouldn't ruin everything between her and Dylan.

Oh, God, it's not fair. Jess moaned as she lay back on the bed, clutching her pillow to her chest. If I didn't have this dumb cancer I could almost believe that I was one of the luckiest people in the world. She smiled as her mind wandered back to that afternoon behind the gum tree. She had felt sort of scared and really shy about kissing Dylan, but it had happened so easily. And what he'd said to her had been so unexpected.

They'd been talking about normal stuff, and then she'd noticed that he was staring at her in a strange way – he was really staring straight into her eyes – and she was staring back at him. He'd just sort of blurted it out. He told her that he really liked her and that he couldn't have imagined liking someone this much. And then they'd kissed. It was that easy. No bumbling or puckering up or slobber or squinty eyes or anything. They'd just been talking one minute, and were kissing the next. Jess hadn't really known what to say back to him – he'd taken her by surprise and she could hardly breathe, she was so happy – so she'd smiled a big smile and squeezed both his hands in hers.

If anyone had told her it might be like this she would have gone all goopy and felt awkward. But it had been nothing like a soppy movie. Thank goodness. The only part that had been even remotely movie-like-romantic had been after the actual kiss, when he had tucked her hair behind her ear. And he had left a splodge of car grease on her face because his hands were still dirty from work, and had thought that this was very funny. So Jess had wiped the excess grease off her face and stuck her finger in his ear. She'd accidentally pushed in a little too far, and could feel the wax. Yuck! Normally, she would have been grossed out. But she hadn't even cared.

She had been on some strange sort of high that had made her want to act impulsively. So she had ripped the cap off Dylan's head and flung it into the air. He had been surprised, but grinned like a cheshire cat. It landed on the end of a long skinny branch of the gum tree and wouldn't come down even when they had both shaken the tree. So Jess had climbed up to retrieve it.

And when they'd walked home later, they'd held

hands and Jess couldn't even remember who'd taken whose hand first. It would have been sickening if it wasn't happening to her personally – if she was reading about it or someone else was telling her this story.

But it had all been so natural. Nothing like Jess had anticipated. There was something about Dylan that made him easy to be with. An honesty. It was what had first caught her attention when she used to watch him in the days before he'd left school. Before they'd ever spoken to one another. It was his honesty and his smile that she really liked. It also helped that he was absolutely gorgeous.

There was a bit of a mystery, though, around why Dylan had gone to work with his father at the garage as soon as he turned fifteen. He'd left school, even though he'd been doing well. And he was intelligent, although you'd never get him to admit it. Jess hadn't asked Dylan about his father because she didn't want him to think that she was prying. It seemed to Jess that there was something about his father that Dylan was keeping very much to himself. And she didn't want to be pushy or make him feel uncomfortable. Jess was discovering – a little more each day – how it felt to be vulnerable or exposed.

She didn't want Dylan to feel like that. And most of all, if he told her about his situation, it would make her feel even more guilty about lying to him. Because no matter how hard she tried to convince herself otherwise, whichever way she looked at this there was one thing that she could not escape. She was lying. By not telling him the truth about her illness, she was lying. So they both had a secret.

They were even.

Chapter 6

The Second Treatment

Beep . . . beep . . . beep . . . beep.

Jess's machine was signalling that it was empty. If they don't hurry up and change this bag, my bladder will burst before I get to the loo, she thought as she sat in the chemotherapy day unit.

She was hooked up – via a needle in her arm – to what looked like a six-pack of beer. If only it *were* beer, my life would be much easier, she thought to herself. Not that she entertained grand dreams of becoming an alcoholic, but this chemotherapy cocktail was pretty extreme stuff. It knocked Jess about severely for days.

'Coming, Jess.'

The nurse came over with a smile and changed

the bag of chemicals that were being fed into Jess's arm intravenously. Jess didn't even flinch when the needle went in. She could watch the whole procedure without turning away. She just wiggled her toes and focused on them.

'Thanks. I have to go to the toilet.'

'OK, can you get up?'

Going to the bathroom with a drip and a six-pack in tow was something akin to Chinese water torture. Jess's pee was red from the chemo, and it stank and made her feel nauseous. And that was on a good day. It wasn't really the sort of thing that you would casually drop into conversation with friends – 'Oh, I've just done this really huge and stinky red piss.'

But it was amazing to witness the fascination of the hospital staff with her bodily functions. They always wanted to know what was happening – where, how much, for how long.

Whoa. Jess was overcome by dizziness. She swooned and swayed, just managing to press the buzzer for help before jamming her right cheek against the wall of the cubicle in an effort to keep herself upright. She sang, trying to stay conscious. Doo wa diddy diddy dum did . . . A male nurse appeared at the door. Oh no. She hadn't pulled her undies up.

Jess didn't even have the strength to feel embarrassed. Maybe that was a good thing. There was nothing she could do about it, anyway.

The nurse was very kind. He pulled her knickers up for her without a comment and sat her in a wheelchair. Then he wheeled her back to the ward and found an unoccupied bed for her to rest in while the treatment finished.

It took about six hours to complete a session. Jess would spend the time reading, or picking the edible bits out of the hospital sandwiches, or talking to other patients, or listening to music, or watching television. She also drank loads of water. Mostly, though, she sat and watched the rhythmic drip, drip, drip as each drop of liquid made its way from the plastic bag, down the tubing and into her vein.

She tried to imagine it to be the clear, healing water of a mountain stream coursing through her entire body, bringing with it a sense of renewed energy and extra life and vitality.

Jess opened her eyes, to see her mother sitting beside the bed. She hadn't even heard the clomping of Ruby's high-heeled shoes making their way up the corridor. She must have been really out of it. Spud was sitting in the vinyl-covered lounge chair beside the bed with one leg draped over the side. He was absorbed in his Game Boy, so much so that he hadn't even touched the very chocolatey-looking milkshake that sat beside him. It must be late, thought Jess, if Spud's finished school already.

Four thirty-five. Hospital clocks were so big that you could see them from any position in the ward. This particular clock was etched into Jess's memory. She had spent hours studying it. She knew it upside down and back to front. She squinted and sort of turned her head. She could still see the clock.

The old man in the bed next to her farted. Spud raised an eyebrow but didn't look up. Ruby stifled a giggle. Jess held her nose.

Finally, the last bag in the six-pack was empty. The nurse removed the needle and Jess felt a small sense of freedom. It was great to be able to walk by herself, even slowly and giddily, to the loo. She set off for the bathroom – and threw up in the toilet.

Two treatments down. Four to go. Almost at the halfway mark. Jess was thankful at least that she did not have to stay overnight in hospital to have her chemo. That was one of the good things about the type of cancer Jess had. Some of the other patients had to stay in for weeks at a time.

In the car on the way home, Jess threw up again on the side of the freeway.

Spud was singing at the top of his lungs, to cover the noise of her heaving.

'Your singing makes me feel even more like puking,' said Jess as she dragged her weary body back into the passenger seat and wiped her tear-stained cheeks and bloodshot eyes with the back of her hand.

'Yeah, yeah. Just hold your guts until we get home, chunderhead,' said Spud. He could be so eloquent sometimes.

'Are you right to go now, sweet pea?' asked Ruby as she directed the dinosaur of a Volkswagen station wagon back into the traffic. Jess was still trying to pull the door shut. Three cars honked their horns at Ruby. One guy stuck his middle finger up and yelled obscenities as he drove past. Jess and Spud sank further into their respective seats. Ruby just smiled, shook her head and took another bite of her salami sandwich. Jess was dreaming of bed. She pulled her woolly hat tightly over her ears and tried to keep her mind off her stomach. Which was pretty hard with the stench of salami wafting across from the driver's seat.

Think light thoughts. Twinkies. Flowers. Fluffy white clouds. Vegetarians. The car jumped forward with a jerky gear change. Jess's stomach churned. She gritted her teeth. An eternity passed.

And finally, she was at home in bed.

Chapter 7

Into a
Black Hole

'No, Sara. She's asleep right now. It was a rough afternoon for her . . . We're OK. It's a very testing time . . . I don't think she'll be at school for a few more days . . . Her blood count is down again . . . Mmmm, it's very low. That means she has little immunity . . . Oh, yes, she's fine . . . Everything is going as it's supposed to . . . Yes, yes – of course I'll tell her you rang . . . Leave it for a few days . . . I know she'd love to see you too . . . All right, Sara, it's always lovely talking to you . . . We'll see you soon . . . Yes, I'm looking forward to it . . . I'm really enjoying getting to know you . . . OK, love . . . goodbye.'

A click. Ruby had put the telephone receiver

down. Her mother had been sucking up to her best friend.

Was nothing sacred?

Jess's life was disappearing before her very eyes.

Being sucked into a black hole.

Damn.

Chapter 8

What If
I Die?

'Jess, your toenails are so strange. They've gone sort of thick and chunky.'

'Tell me about it. I think it must be the chemo. My fingernails are a bit weird too. Look.' She held out her hands. Sara studied them for a moment.

'Mmm. They're sort of yellowy, but not as noticeable as your toes.'

'Yuck, aren't they?'

'They're OK. If keeping you alive means cobbly old toenails for a while, I reckon you got a good deal.' Sara took a deep breath. 'Jess, I know you feel pretty terrible and this probably isn't a good time, but I have to say it. I think you should tell Dylan you're sick. He's been asking about you every day

43

and I'm running out of different things to tell him.'

Jess exhaled slowly. She had been expecting this conversation. 'Sara, you're so great at making up stories. The best.'

'That's not the point, Jess.'

Jess needed to buy some more time. She had to convince Sara to keep up the charade for a bit longer, at least.

'What about with Mrs Minerva the other day when you were carrying on about washing lines and seaweed in Japan? She totally forgot about the question she'd asked by the time you'd finished confusing her.'

'Jess, that's different. Mrs Minerva isn't snogging my best friend and dying to see her again cos she seems to have disappeared off the face of the planet . . . Unless there's something you haven't told me.'

'Don't be an idiot.' Jess chucked her pillow at Sara. It missed.

'Far be it from me to stand between a bald, skinny, drop-dead gorgeous sixteen-year-old and her ancient human development teacher if that's what – '

'Sara. Stop.'

'You know she could be put away for life. Gross! Could you imagine?'

'Shut up.' Jess was having a hard time trying to keep her lunch down.

'All right.' Sara glanced at Jess. 'I still think you should tell Dylan you're sick. It's not fair.'

'I know. But it's just not that easy. I can't.'

'Jess, I feel awful about this. For you and for him. But now I'm starting to feel sorry for myself too. I hate lying, and I don't even think he believes me half the time any more. He's smart, you know.'

'Yeah, I know.'

'Well, it's getting hard for me to look him in the face, you know, and lie to him and stuff. You have to tell him. He's nuts about you. And I don't want him to hate me.'

'I know. I want to. I will, I'm trying. I really want to. It's just so hard.'

'Jess, more kids at school know. I don't know how, but they're finding out. I haven't told them – '

'I know that, Sara.'

'You can't keep this secret for ever, Jess. Dylan will find out one day – whether you tell him or not.'

'Yeah, that's what Spud said too.'

'Well, Spud's right. And so am I.'

'Sara, this is so hard. I want to. I really want to.'

'Well then, just do it.'

'But I have to have some normal time as well.'

'What do you mean?'

'I just need to do normal things and be, well, normal. I don't know how to explain it.' Tears were collecting in the corners of Jess's eyes. 'Everyone treats me like I have to be wrapped up in cotton wool or something. You should have seen the stare Mum's friend gave me earlier. It's bad enough looking like a freak, but it's the pits being treated like one too. You heard what that Year Seven kid did. He thought I was contagious. Well, at least he had the guts to say something. It's better than bloody staring. I know people are finding out. Yesterday I walked into a room and the conversation stopped. I knew they were talking about me cos not one of them would even look my way. I haven't suddenly become a mindless idiot.' Jess was sobbing and swallowing gulps of air. She was finding it hard to breathe.

'Jess, calm down. Just relax. I'll get you some water.' Sara was back in ten seconds with a plastic cup and a curly straw.

'Sorry.'

'You don't have to be sorry.' Sara stared at her friend, wringing her hands and not quite sure of where to put her feet. 'Jess, what do I do now? What can I do? Can I help?'

'Just treat me like I'm bloody-well normal. That's all I want.' Jess let out a huge, frustrated sigh. 'Did you know that Charlotte hasn't spoken to me for a whole week? She hasn't rung me or e-mailed me or even sent a text message. Nothing. She thinks I'm a freak or something.'

Sara was quiet. She did know about Charlotte.

'You and Dylan are the only normal things in my life at the moment. That might sound totally stupid but it's how I feel. Mum just cries at everything and then lights her incense. And I hate lying to Dylan. It's the worst thing in the world. But if I tell him the truth, what will happen?'

'I don't know. You're not going to know either, until you try.'

'But that's just it, I don't know. I don't want him to drop me. I don't want him to feel sorry for me. I just want this all to go away.'

'Well, you're almost halfway through your treatment.'

47

'Yeah, so what?' Jess picked the flaky bits off her nail polish. She flicked them at Sara.

'Rack off.' Sara grinned and flicked them back.

Ruby was vacuuming the passage outside the door, a distant hum. The girls were both quiet for a moment.

'I'm scared, Sara.'

'Of what?'

'What if I die? I'll be so pissed off if I die. Especially now, like, with Dylan and everything.'

'I can't even think about you dying. You just won't.'

'Nah, not this week anyway.' Jess half grinned.

'I should hope not.' They were both quiet for a while. Sara looked like she had something on her mind.

'So, Jess, have you and Dylan . . . ?'

'What?'

'Have you . . . Did you . . . Oh, don't worry.'

'What?' Jess was enjoying watching Sara squirm a bit. And it was a better conversation than one about dying. Not much easier, though.

Sara and Jess were very similar when it came to talking about sex and stuff – they both became a bit shy and quiet. Unlike Charlotte. If Charlotte had been here that would have been the first thing she'd have asked. 'So, Jess, what's he like?' And she would have laughed her gravelly smoker's laugh and they would have gossiped about it for ages. But Charlotte wasn't here.

'Oh, Jess, it's none of my business. I just wondered if you and Dylan had . . . Oh, forget it. I don't even really want to know.'

That was an outright lie. Sara was clearly bursting to know.

'You want to know if we've done it?' Jess asked.

Sara looked a bit sheepish. And very interested. She nodded.

'Jeez, Sara. Look at me. I haven't even got the strength to pick my own nose sometimes.'

'Have you thought about it?'

'Sara!'

'Well, have you? You must have. He's gorgeous. If you're thinking about death and stuff you must be thinking about this as well.'

'All right, yes, I have. But I'm not going to jump up and do it just because I might die tomorrow . . .'

Jess stopped in mid-sentence. This thought had

only just occurred to her. Her heart skipped a beat. What if she died a virgin?

'Hang on. Maybe I should just do it. It's not as if I'll get pregnant or anything. You probably can't when you're on chemo. Yeah, maybe I should just go and bonk Dylan right now and be done with it. Nothing to lose, hey.'

Jess's lips formed a tight line. Suddenly she was angry. And sad. And confused. All at once.

'Sorry I brought it up,' said Sara.

'This whole situation sucks. That's why I can't tell Dylan I'm sick. Everything changes once people know. Everything. I don't want him to think I'm with him because I just want to bonk someone before I die. Maybe it would be easier if I just died right now.'

'You don't – '

'No, I don't mean that.' Jess was exhausted.

'You'd better bloody not.' Sara looked angry. This was too much. She got up and began rearranging the books on the shelf, which was what she always did when she didn't know what else to do.

Jess began to speak. 'They're in alphabetical order . . .'

'I don't care. Anyway, you won't need them if

you're going to die tomorrow. That was a really dumb thing to say, Jess.'

'Sorry, Sara,' said Jess softly. 'That wasn't fair.'

'No, it wasn't. It wasn't a fair thing to say. I hate that you said it and made me get mad at you because now I feel guilty. It was a stupid thing to say.'

'I know. I just got carried away. Sometimes I just start feeling sorry for myself.'

'Jess, I want to do whatever I can, you know? But this isn't easy for me either.'

'I know it's not. Thanks, Sara. For everything. I don't know what I'd do without you.'

'Yeah, well. Just don't die or anything stupid.'

'I'll do my best.'

Something got stuck in the vacuum cleaner at the other end of the house. Ruby swore.

Sara looked sideways at Jess and caught her eye. They both smiled. Ruby's language could be very colourful.

'Are you OK?'

'Yep. Are you?'

'Yep.'

'What are you thinking about now?'

Jess rolled over. 'That even if I was close to dying

51

– like, even closer than I am now – I wouldn't bonk Dylan just so I'd done it once in my life. I don't think I would, anyway. I don't know. I just wouldn't want anything else in the way. If we did it. Does that make sense?'

Sara nodded. 'You really like him, don't you?'

'Yep.'

There was a silence. Both girls were inside their own thoughts.

'Jess?'

'Mmmm?'

'I don't think it's your time to die yet.'

'I hope not.'

'I hope not too. I'd miss you too much.'

'Snap.'

That was Jess's way of saying 'Me too'.

Chapter 9

The
Letter

Jess stared at the ceiling for a long time after Sara left. Her mind was racing with so many ideas that it was hard to make sense of any of them.

One thing, however, kept returning to the front of her thoughts. Jess knew that she had to do something about Dylan. Sara was right. Jess couldn't expect her to keep on lying to him. It wasn't fair on anyone. But what could she do?

She thought for a few more minutes. Then, with a sense of urgency, she reached over and picked up the writing paper that was on her bedside table.

Dear Dylan,
I'm just writing to say that I think you're a really nice guy and

Nice. What did that word 'nice' mean anyway? It sounded way too insipid.

> Dear Dylan,
> Although you're the best thing that's ever happened to me in my entire life, there's something that might come between us

Too gushy? Too emotional?

> Dear Dylan,
> I've been lying to you for weeks on end, and making my friends and family lie to you as well. I've been missing school and avoiding you because I've got cancer and I'm in the middle of having treatment

Damn it.

> Dear Dylan,
> I won't blame you if you hate me for what you're about to find out, but I need you to know that there are reasons for the choice that I made not to tell you sooner

> Dear Dylan,
> It's been nice knowing you but I can't see you any more

The Letter

Dear Dylan,

You are wonderful. But for my own stupid and selfish reasons I can't see you any more. It's not something I can talk about at the moment, but I hope that in time you might understand and forgive me. It's not you – you are fun and kind and I have enjoyed being with you so much that I can't describe it. It's me. I have some stuff to work out. And I don't want to drag you into it. I'm sorry. More than you can know.

Goodbye

Love, Jess

She debated about whether to write 'love' at the end and finally she thought, Stuff it, and put it in. That was how she felt. Damn it. Stupid cancer.

She poked the letter into an envelope and scribbled his address on the front. If she didn't go out and post it right away, she probably never would.

It was one of the hardest decisions of her life. She hoped that it was the right one. She would have to be strong in her convictions and follow through the decision she made.

She wouldn't see Dylan at all. She wouldn't talk

to him on the telephone. She would stop all communication with him. Jess took a deep breath, gave the back of the envelope a kiss for a safe journey, and walked down the street to the post office.

Jess forced herself to believe that it was better this way. No emotional scenes. No breaking down in tears. And besides, Jess didn't trust herself to keep her secret in the heat of an emotional confrontation with Dylan. Anyone else, but not Dylan. It was almost like he could see through her.

Jess made a list in her mind. This was the right thing to do because she wouldn't have to lie to his face any more. And he wouldn't have to make the difficult decision of whether or not to stay in a relationship with a girl who might cark it soon. Or who might throw up on him while they were at the pictures. Or black out while they were rollerblading.

She swept aside the feelings of guilt that were beginning to creep into her head, and reminded herself that she didn't want Dylan to feel sorry for her. Or feel like he had to hang around with her because she was sick.

This was the best way. Jess tried hard to convince

herself. It was best for everyone. For Sara. For Spud. For Dylan. The best way.

She wiped a stray tear from her cheek and posted the letter. Then she abruptly turned on her heel and walked quickly back up the street, hoping that she wouldn't bump into anyone she knew.

Chapter 10

Her Own
Funeral

Jess woke up in a cold sweat. Her pjs were sodden with perspiration. Damn it. This hadn't happened for ages. Not since she'd started chemotherapy, anyway. Did this mean it wasn't working? Night sweats were one of the symptoms that had led to her being diagnosed with cancer. Along with a whole lot of other stuff.

At times like this, Jess couldn't keep herself from imagining the worst. That the chemotherapy was doing nothing. That all this treatment was for nothing. That the cancer had taken over the rest of her body and nobody knew. Even the doctors wouldn't know if the treatment had been successful until it was finished. And the only way of knowing,

58

even then, would be to monitor Jess for many more years to check that the cancer didn't recur. There were no guarantees.

Jess had times when she didn't give a stuff about the cancer, and times when she was so scared that she just wished she was a little girl again and nothing could hurt her.

Her family had had happy moments. It hadn't been all beer and skittles, but these happier memories helped when Jess needed reminding that there was goodness in the world.

Sometimes she would pick up her pillow, make her way softly down the passage and crawl into Ruby's bed. Just to feel the warmth of her body. The familiarity of the loud and regular tick, tick, tick of the bedside clock. She had always felt so safe in this big bed. Like nothing in the world could touch her. Even Ruby's snoring didn't matter at these times. It was just nice to nestle in and feel secure.

Jess took off her damp pyjamas and shivered. Her body was covered with goosebumps. She found a big old jumper that her dad had left behind, which she had saved from the rag-bag. Ruby had gone through the wardrobe after a few years had gone by and Dad still hadn't come back, throwing out virtually everything. Except the jumper.

Jess pulled open her curtains and curled up under the duvet. The moon was almost full. She wasn't tired. Her mind was racing.

Slowly and rhythmically, Jess began to rock backwards and forwards. Small movements. Just enough to ease the pain from the tumour she was feeling in her shoulder and comfort herself at the same time. The pain didn't seem to be easing since chemo. She hummed. A little song that her mother used to sing to her when she was frightened of the dark night.

The moon glowed brightly through the big tree in the backyard, casting shadows on to her bedroom wall. Jess smiled as she thought back to Dylan and the gum tree. His hat. His grin. His warmth. She wondered what he was doing at that moment. Whether he thought about her much. How he felt about the letter.

Her pain was easing now and she was feeling a bit warmer. The back of her neck was still damp so she put on her cotton hat. She could feel the chill in the air and didn't want to catch another cold. She'd had enough of those already.

Eleven-thirty. Friday night. Charlotte and Sara and the others would be out somewhere – rollerblading or at the movies or down at the beach with a bonfire in a rusty old bin. Those were the nights that Jess loved. Just sitting outside, listening to the pounding of the surf on the beach and feeling the warmth of the flames on your face and your front. And when your back got too cold, you'd just turn around and 'cook' your other side.

Sometimes the others would sneak a bottle of booze on to the beach, but mostly they just talked. Charlotte smoked her lungs out, of course, and they would play stuff like charades or Truth or Dare. Then they would solve the problems of the world and dream about what they would be doing in five years' time.

Five years' time. Suddenly that seemed a very long way off.

Would Jess still be alive?

Her mind flitted from the dancing waves and swirling surf to her imagining own funeral. This was so weird. Not scary, really, but *so* weird.

Jess was still awake, but felt like she was dreaming. She was lying in a coffin in her favourite scarlet dress and she looked incredibly peaceful. Almost beautiful. She probably *would* have used the word beautiful if it were someone else she was describing. And the image she saw made it seem as though she were asleep, or in a trance.

The service was being held on the beach and the tide was coming in, leaving great white streaks of foam on the golden sand. Everything was moving in slow motion. The women wore flowing dresses which billowed as a gentle wind caressed the shore and whispered secrets to the guests.

She could see everyone very clearly – especially their faces. There was her mother and Spud. And Sara, Charlotte and Joffa, and all the other kids from school. A little further away on a craggy rock was Dylan with his arms outstretched, and her father was at the playground nearby with a clown suit on and fake dog poo that he was using to make all the children laugh. There were hundreds of little kids. Suddenly, the whole gathering of people rose to their feet and began to sing a mournful, beautiful song, in harmony. The waves were crashing on to the shore and getting larger as the water encroached on the assembled group. Everyone was being covered in a fine salty mist from the giant spray.

And then, in the middle of the final chorus, Jess arose from the coffin like some mystical scarlet angel risen from the deep. She floated above everyone, soaring with the rhythm of the wind and the ocean. They all stared, open-mouthed. No one said a word.

Finally, she gathered armfuls of rose petals from a silver-coloured bag, and showered them on to the guests. And then, leaving them with these red, fragrant memories of her, she disappeared on the crest of a glorious wave and on to the great beyond. And that was that.

Wow. What a spin out!

Jess rolled over. She hoped that if she did die soon, that at least they'd play some decent music. Maybe she should write a will or something. *Please do not play shonky music at my funeral.* And she'd have to leave her things to people. Not that she had many worldly possessions. One pair of rollerblades. That was about it, really. But she would hate for them to sing really mournful songs at her funeral. Maybe she should just tell her mum that.

She thought the beach location was pretty cool, though. It had an air of joy as well as sadness about it. And it was one of Jess's favourite places. In fact, everything about that dream sequence was pretty spot on, except for the music. And, of course, the fact that she wasn't dead yet.

Wow. She didn't even feel goopy or anything! In fact, she was elated in a funny kind of way.

Her own funeral!

Chapter 11

It's Hard for Friends Too

Charlotte didn't show up. She had arranged to meet Sara so they'd come over together, then, she'd rung with some vague excuse about shopping with Joffa for mag wheels. Jess was really pissed off at first.

'Jess, Charlotte's just trying to stay cool, you know. She does everything for Joffa . . .'

'You don't have to make excuses for her, Sara. God, I just can't believe it. It's been two weeks.'

'Yeah, well, she's . . .' Sara's idea seemed to evaporate into nothing. She had no more excuses.

'She's decided not to hang around. Full stop,' said Jess. She wasn't going to beat around the bush any more.

'Well, look on the bright side. Joffa's car is gleaming with all the crappy new parts they've been shopping for lately,' said Sara.

'I hope the chrome exhaust backfires. And that those stupid wipers scratch his windscreen. And I'd just love to tell him where he could shove his fluffy dice.'

Sara began to giggle. It was contagious. Jess couldn't help herself. Soon they were both letting out big throaty guffaws and chuckling like there was no tomorrow.

In between fits of laughter, Sara said, 'Charlotte told me this story about Joffa. He went to get a new tune for his car horn and was given the wrong one. He was being so cool and tough until he got road rage, smashed his hand to the steering wheel and the horn played "On the Good Ship Lollipop"!'

Jess was snorting with laughter. 'Why didn't he check it when he bought it?'

'I think Charlotte was narked at him for something and they'd had a row. He was a bit distracted.'

'That is so tragic.'

'I know. He made Charlotte swear on her mother's grave that she wouldn't tell his mates.'

It wasn't even that funny, but they rolled around the floor for ages, cackling like hens and with tears streaming from their eyes. It was one of those moments where if they even looked at one another they'd be set off again.

After ten minutes they'd recovered. Mostly. Jess was still holding her stomach, which convulsed every now and then of its own volition.

'You want to know something else that's funny?' Sara asked.

'What?' A few stray giggles were still escaping from Jess. It was ace. She hadn't laughed so hard for ages.

'Charlotte's worried about you dying, so she can't face hanging around any more while you're alive.'

'Oh, that's hysterical, Sara.'

'But doesn't it strike you as funny? Like, not funny ha-ha, but just funny in Charlotte's weirdo way?'

'It's about as funny as a fart under a duvet.'

Jess lunged for her own duvet, which she shoved under Sara's nose. Sara swiped her away with both arms and whacked her with the pillow. No special treatment here.

'Or a hole in the head.'

Jess's giggles were finally coming to a halt. She rearranged her woolly hat. It was itchy because her head was hot, so she stuck it on the bedpost. It still felt strange not having her hair tickle her neck.

Jess wasn't giving up. 'Even if she felt like that, and that's a big if, I still can't believe that she won't come around or anything. How does she think I feel, knowing that she thinks I'm going to drop dead? It's all pretty stuffed, if you ask me.'

'Yeah, it's all pretty stuffed.' Sara twiddled the ring on her middle finger. She paused for a moment as if she was trying to choose her words carefully. 'You know, Jess, I can sort of understand where Charlotte's coming from. It would be easier in some ways not to see you. I don't mean cos you're a noof or anything, but just because it's really hard sometimes to know what to say and what to do.'

'That's crap, Sara.'

'It's true, Jess. It can be really hard. Sometimes I have to, like, sit down and take a few breaths before I come in to see you.'

'You're kidding me, right?'

'No, I'm not.'

'Why? What do you mean?'

'If I don't know what's happened with you, or even sometimes how you might look on a certain day. It can be a real surprise to come in and see you ghostly pale or throwing up or whatever. Jess, don't look at me like that.'

Jess was giving Sara one of her more intensive stares.

Sara bravely continued. 'This is really hard to say, but I just think you should know that I can relate to how Charlotte's feeling, in a funny kind of way.'

'I think you're full of it.'

'Jess, it's true. Remember that kid who got half his face torn off in that bike accident, and how it was really hard to look at him and he stayed away from school for ages afterwards?'

'Yeah. Jamie Muldoon. What's he got to do with it?'

'It's sort of the same kind of thing. Someone's sick. Looks really different to how they used to look. You're at school one day, and then you're not. One day you're firing jokes left, right and centre, and the next you're throwing up all over your folder. It's just hard to hang around with someone who's so . . . so . . . fragile or something. It's hard to explain.'

'So are you saying that you'd rather not visit me any more?'

'No, you dopey fart. I'm just saying that it can be hard for your friends too. I know it's harder for you.'

Jess was thoughtful for a moment. Then, quite slowly and deliberately, she said, 'Sara, I think I really might die if I didn't have you to talk to. I don't want you to get a big head or anything, cos heaven knows it's big enough already.'

'Watch it, baldy.'

'Yeah, yeah. Well . . . just . . . thanks for being my friend even though I've lost my devastating good looks and you have to do heavy breathing before you see me.'

'It's all right. I know I'm just one of those special people who goes around lightening the hearts of those who –'

'Shut up.'

'OK. But try not to be too annoyed with Charlotte. She might get over this soon, and then maybe things can get back to normal.'

'Whatever "normal" is.'

Jess looked over at Sara. 'Did Charlotte actually say that? That she's worried about me dying?'

'Sort of,' Sara replied. 'She didn't have to say it all. I could just tell from what she didn't say. You know?'

For a moment there was silence.

'Yeah,' Jess said. 'I know.'

Chapter 12

After the Third Treatment

As the days inched slowly by, Jess found it easier not to count them any more.

She felt that she was on a mental merry-go-round. At times her mind would become obsessed with chemotherapy routines and the whole cancer thing. Then it would turn to Dylan, and then to school. Over and over again. Chemotherapy, Dylan, school, Charlotte, her family. Up and down and around on the merry-go-round. No escape. No change of music. Just an infernal, never-ending, maddening cacophony inside her head. Time was passing around her. But she was in limbo. Suspended animation.

Everyone else was going about living their own lives and hers was on hold.

She couldn't do anything. The chemotherapy was knocking her about badly.

Jess longed for an escape. A distraction for her mind.

School was a write-off. She had no powers of concentration. No energy. She wasn't even attempting to go. In fact, she had missed so much school now that she would probably have to repeat Year Eleven. She couldn't read the assignment sheets that Sara brought round without waves of nausea pounding over her. It wasn't fair.

Physically, she was suffering a lot. She felt disgusting all the time. From the vomiting to the mouth ulcers and the constant flu-like symptoms, to the wicked lethargy and her very bald head, she felt disgusting.

And there was Dylan. Jess felt even more sick in the stomach when she thought about him. She hadn't heard anything from him since she'd sent the letter over two weeks ago. Nothing. Even though she had told herself she'd have to cut off all communication with him, she was still hurt and surprised that he hadn't even tried to contact her. It was an ego thing. A pride thing. If he'd really liked her he would have at least tried. Wouldn't he?

73

Chapter 13

The Interrogation

Sara came bursting into Jess's place, panting and out of breath.

'Jess, you'll never guess what's happened.'

'What?'

'I was just at the bus stop minding my own business when Dylan rocks up with Mike.'

Jess jokingly called Mike 'Dylan's stooge' because he looked like a bodyguard and was so protective. Once, she had tried to talk about it with Dylan but he just got totally embarrassed and changed the subject.

Sara continued. 'Anyway, I said g'day to Dylan, like I usually do, and sort of smiled at Mike, cos I never know what to say to him. He doesn't talk much, does he?'

'Nope.'

'How come?' Sara asked.

'I dunno. Maybe he thinks no one will listen. That's why he hangs around with Dylan.'

'I've never really heard him talk until today.'

'I don't think I ever have, either. Even when Dylan tries to include him in conversations he goes really shy.'

'Anyway, anyway. Let me tell you about what happened. The only thing Dylan says to me is "How's Jess?" So I say, "She's OK." And then, I couldn't believe what happened next. Mike comes up to me. And the same Mike who never speaks is, like, really close, with absolutely no idea of personal space, and he says, "So, what's the deal with your mate dropping Dylan?"

'And of course, I say, "I don't know what you're talking about" and I'm trying to get away from the fine spray of spit that's landing on me cos he's so close. Then he says again, "Come on, she's your best friend, isn't she? Tell us. What's the deal? Has she got someone else?"

'So of course I say, "No". But there's this really strange vibe happening and I'm starting to feel uneasy. Then he says – get this – he says, "No one upsets my mate and gets away with it. You tell her that. Who does she think she is?" And Dylan pulls him back from me and says, "Shut up, Mike. Don't interfere." And then he says, "Sorry, Sara, Mike just gets a bit worked up sometimes." But he won't even look at me. No eye contact. Nothing. So weird. And not like Dylan at all.

'So then, as you can imagine, I'm silently willing him to look at me but his eyes don't budge, and stud-jacket-boy is about to start in again with the interrogation, so I have to think on my feet. And what I'm thinking is, this is some weird sort of hokey stuff going down and I've gotta get out of here and talk to Jess. So, I go for the usual and launch into, "Um . . . ah . . . I've gotta go now – sore stomach. It just came on.' Then, I immediately sprint over to my best friend's house to find out exactly what is going on.'

'And now here you are.'

Jess had been unable to get a word in edgeways until now. Not that she had to say much. Her guilt-ridden face was giving her away.

'Jess, what's going on?'

Jess couldn't answer.

'In my head, I know that you wouldn't have done something so stupid as to drop Dylan.'

Jess felt like Sara's penetrating gaze might bore a hole right through her. She could see that the truth was beginning to dawn on her friend.

'And I also know that, as my best friend, you'd tell me straight away if you *had* dropped Dylan. There's no way you'd break up with him without telling me. Because you wouldn't want to put me in such a horrible situation. Would you?'

Jess couldn't even look at Sara.

'Jess, it's true, isn't it?'

Jess just nodded.

Sara held her head in her hands. 'I can't believe you'd put me on the spot like that, Jess. I've lied through my teeth to save your butt and now you go and do something like this without even thinking to warn me. For God's sake, Jess, I see the guy at the bus stop all the time.'

'I'm sorry.'

'You're sorry?'

'Sara, what can I say? I'm sorry. I'm really sorry. I just couldn't think of any other way. I didn't even think about what it might do to you.' Jess was in tears. Suddenly she looked really vulnerable.

Sara's tone became softer. But she still seemed pretty mad. 'Oh, Jess, you can't have broken up with him. Why would you do that? Please tell me this is all a bad dream. You're kidding me, right?' Sara looked pleadingly at her friend.

'No, I'm not kidding.'

'Damn it, Jess. Do you think this will fix everything? Make it all better? I've just acted like a complete blockhead in front of him, but he wouldn't have noticed if I'd jumped off a cliff. All he can think about is you. The guy's devastated. You should see him.'

'Do you think I'm doing cartwheels across the floor? It's not as if I had much choice.' Jess hurled her slipper at the wall.

Sara slumped on to the bed. 'I can't believe you did this. I don't understand. I've *lied* for you. I can't believe it. Dylan's crazy about you. Nutso. Crazy.'

'Believe it.' Jess had curled herself into the foetal position.

'I can't. I think this cancer's gone to your head.'

'Probably.'

They sat, not saying anything, for a while. Jess reached for the tissue box. Sara grabbed a trashy magazine that was lying on the floor and distractedly started flicking through it. Neither of them said anything for a long time.

Finally, Sara broke the ice. 'So, how about Mike – is he for real or what? It's like he thinks he's a nightclub bouncer. And the attitude – unbelievable. I couldn't work out what his story was.'

'I know. It's like Dylan's his hero or something. He does whatever Dylan asks him to do without batting an eyelid.'

'Urgh. It's sort of creepy. I felt really strange with him. It was kind of like he was trying to chat me up but I felt almost threatened at the same time. He made the hairs on the back of my neck stand up. A real loser.'

'Tell me about it, Sara. I couldn't think of anything more gross than doing the wicked wild thing with him.'

'Even when he doesn't talk he makes my skin crawl.'

'Yeah, I think lots of people feel that way about him.' Jess thought for a moment and then continued. 'It's sad. I know he seems a bit weird. But I think he's harmless enough. From what Dylan's said, I don't think Mike has much to do, or has much of a home life, either. He always hangs around at Dylan's dad's workshop. And he's pretty good with cars. Maybe cos he doesn't have to talk to them.'

'Mmmm. Trust Dylan to look out for him,' Sara said, smiling. 'It's still hard to believe they're mates.'

'I know. Dylan helped him out somehow – like, years ago, and he's just hung around since. He means well, I think.'

'It didn't really feel that way to me. But I hope so anyway.'

'So do I. Sara, I am sorry. I should have told you about splitting up with Dylan.'

'Yeah, well, anyway. It's getting late. I have to go now and help Mum. That's if I can make it. Apparently I've got an unbelievably bad stomach-ache. Thanks to you.'

Sara moved towards the door, clutching her stomach as she had done earlier that afternoon, to go and help at her mother's roadside flower stall. She paused dramatically, swivelled on one leg, turned in the doorway and, in a very posh voice said, 'One good thing may come from all this acting. I'll probably get an "A" for drama this year.'

'You would have got an "A" for drama whether I had cancer or not,' said Jess, smiling.

'Whatever.' Sara turned back to Jess with one more observation. 'I honestly never imagined you'd do something like break up with Dylan. It's such a shock.'

'I know. I just couldn't lie to him any more. I had no choice.'

'I think deep down I know why you did it, Jess. But there's always a choice.'

'You sound like my mother. Go and sell a flower or something.'

'I will. Bye.'

Chapter 14

Who the Hell is Rosie?

Still no word from Dylan.

Jess was trying to forget about him, but he seemed to jump into her head at every opportunity. She couldn't shake her thoughts of him.

In her life, everything was getting harder to deal with. Her mother was becoming more and more suffocating, and taking loads of time off work to look after her. In a way, Jess was glad that someone was there to help when her body played tricks on her. She was very weak and had been catching every cold and flu that was going. But it was impossible to stay sane without any privacy. No time to herself when she needed it. She was trapped inside her body. And worse still, she didn't know if this body of hers would last much longer.

Jess shivered. She hated thinking about dying. It scared her. The great unknown. She didn't have a faith. She wasn't particularly religious or anything. She had been to church a couple of times with friends at Christmas, but that was it. She did believe in God. Or she thought she did, most of the time anyway. She held her father's beliefs when it came to the Almighty – that it would be just too stupid for nearly everyone in the world to believe in some sort of God if one didn't exist at all. But there were times when she questioned the existence of an almighty being. Especially when things on Earth became so freaky. Like now.

Sara kept bringing strange stories from the outside world into Jess's bedroom. The latest saga involved Charlotte. She had been expelled from school for smoking (she'd been caught three times in two days), which was totally dumb because Charlotte was as good as Houdini himself when it came to creating illusions. She could have a smoke at the principal's desk one second before he walked into the room and still not be caught. She was a master magician. This was really odd. The only explanation to make any sense was that she wanted to be caught. But why on earth would she want that?

Jess really wished that she could understand what was going on inside Charlotte's head. It was obvious that their lives were changing. Charlotte could be like a crab at the best of times, protecting herself with a hard outer shell. But this not-visiting-Jess-cos-she-might-die thing was really getting up Jess's nose. It was ridiculous. And Jess missed her, too.

It had been good to talk to Sara about how she really felt. Jess hadn't realised before that it might be hard for some people to visit her when she was sick. She still thought it was pretty dumb but it did make some sense. Not much, but a bit.

Another freaky thing that Jess couldn't get out of her mind was Sara's description of what had happened at the bus stop just that afternoon. She had overheard Dylan talking to Mike. He had said that he was going to pick up Rosie.

Whoever the hell she was.

Poor old broken-hearted Dylan. Would it have killed him to at least wait a bit longer?

And then there was Spud; her little pesky brother.

Day by day, he was becoming more distant and unapproachable. He didn't smile much any more. In fact, he didn't talk much. He just spent hours in his bedroom playing computer games, or bouncing his basketball outside. Even then, he didn't do his own running commentary as he used to do – 'And the crowd roars. It's Spud McAllister, faster than the speed of light. And he's done it AGAIN!' as he leaped into the air and dropped the ball through the hoop over and over again. These days, Jess would just hear the dull thud, thud, thud as he bounced the ball and shot hoops. No fancy footwork. No excited commentary. Just a steady barrage of thuds.

Every day after school, he used to come in and jump on her bed just to annoy her. And secretly, it had been one of the highlights of her day. But lately he had been moody. And there had been no bed trampolining at all. Now he was just snappy and cranky. At first Jess had thought that he was just annoyed at all the attention she was getting. But this seemed different to Spud wanting a present every time Jess had chemo. It seemed to run a lot deeper.

Spud had lost his sparkle. It was like he'd grown up overnight and suddenly become suspicious and wary. He seemed to have lost his innocence. And his eyes sometimes had a look that Jess couldn't pinpoint.

Usually Jess was pretty good at figuring out what was happening to Spud. This time, she had no idea.

Chapter 15

What About Spud?

Jess was not the only one in the family to be concerned about the change in Spud's personality. Ruby was also beginning to suspect that something might be going on.

'Jess, have you noticed anything different about your brother lately?' Before Jess could answer, Ruby fired another question, 'Has he spoken to you at all about anything unusual?'

'What, like aliens landing on the front lawn or the house being overrun by bunny rabbits in little pink tutus?'

'Oh, Jess, it's good to see that you still have that wicked sense of humour. But I need you to be serious. I'm talking about school.'

'What about it?'

'Well, I saw the principal today. I was summoned to his office.'

'Why, what did you do?' Jess was half serious. She was never quite sure what her mother was capable of. 'Oh, Mum, tell me you didn't stick your chewy under his desk.'

Ruby ignored Jess's witty interjection. 'Mr Simpson thinks you're very courageous. In fact, all of your teachers seem to have only positive things to say about your strength and your academic ability.'

'Yeah, yeah. I don't want to talk about me and school, seeing as I haven't even been able to get there for the last twenty-five years.' Jess was still feeling quite depressed about all the school she had missed. 'What about Spud?'

'Well, apparently he's been missing a lot of school. And he hasn't been at all for the last two days. Jess, this is very serious. Do you know anything at all about it?'

Jess was stunned. She shook her head. No. Spud had been riding his bike to school each day as usual. So where was he going, in his uniform, every day? It was dawning on Jess that her intuition had been right all along. Something was really getting at Spud.

Ruby's voice interrupted Jess's thoughts. 'I can see that you're as surprised as I am. He hasn't been his cheerful self lately, has he? I just thought it was all the running about – you know, the hospital visits and things. You don't think he's in trouble do you? On drugs, or taken up with the wrong crowd? I'd never forgive myself if I thought that he'd been reaching out for help and I'd ignored the signs. It's just so hard lately. Oh my goodness, it's my fault. Four times this week – four times – he's had to get his own dinner because I've been at work. It's all my fault. That wretched afternoon shift.'

'Mum, don't.'

'I haven't been giving him the attention he needs. He's crying out for it. I've been so preoccupied.'

'Mum, I'm sure he'll be fine. We just need to find out what's going on. Did Mr Simpson say anything else?'

'Yes – well, no. He sent me to the Pupil Welfare Co-ordinator. Apparently, Spud's been behaving strangely in class as well. Three of his teachers have expressed their concern. Three of them, Jess.'

'We just have to talk to him, Mum.'

'Yes. I wonder where he is. He should have been home by now. Oh, God, do you think I need to call the police?'

'He's only a few minutes late, Mum.'

'You're right.'

'I know.'

'Jess, I really have to pick up this prescription. You're due for another tablet in thirty minutes and we're out of them.'

'You go, Mum.'

'I'm taking the mobile. Promise me you'll ring if you hear from your brother.'

'Yes, Mum.'

'Are you sure you'll be OK?' Jess was looking pale.

'Yes, Mum. I'm big enough and ugly enough to look after myself these days.'

'You know I don't like you talking that way. I'll be back in a jiff.'

As Ruby pulled out of the driveway, Jess heard Spud's bedroom door click shut. He must have snuck in the back way. She listened at his door for a minute, to check that it was her brother and not a robber. Then she tiptoed back to the kitchen to call Ruby and put her mind at ease.

Chapter 16

Stupid Dumb Cancer

Jess knocked on Spud's door. 'Spud, open up.'

'Go away.'

'Spud, Mum's gonna break it down if you don't open up. Just unlock the door and let me in. It won't take long.' Jess had been trying to coax Spud out of his room for a good ten minutes. Even the lure of chocolate wasn't working.

'Nick off!' Spud had had a gut full.

'All right, we'll talk through the door. What's all this crap about you not going to school this week?'

'Leave me alone.'

'Spud, just talk to me, would you? We want to help. Look, Mum's not here at the moment, she's picking up a prescription from the chemist. Won't you at least tell me what's going on?'

'Why should I?'

'Because I care about you and I want to know what's happening.'

'Yeah, right. That's a good one.' Spud snorted with indignation.

'What do you mean, Spud?'

'Yeah, right. It's fine to pretend you care about me now.'

'Spud, I don't know what you're talking about.'

'Well, you obviously didn't care about me very much when you made me swear to keep your secret.'

'Spud.'

'Don't act like you care, Jess. Just stop. I hate you and I don't want to talk to you any more.'

Jess did stop. He'd never said he hated her before. Her stomach lurched. She bit her lip and continued. 'Spud, what secret? Are you talking about my being sick?'

'What do you reckon? I'm not keeping any secrets for the CIA, am I?'

Jess couldn't believe it. First Sara, and now Spud. This dumb idea of keeping her illness a secret. She'd made them both swear that they wouldn't talk about it. She had known that Spud would tell no one. He was a tough little cookie who was ferociously loyal to his big sister, even if they did annoy each other at times. He would die before he would divulge her secret. They were pretty close, especially since their dad had left.

Jess tried again. 'What's happened, Spud?'

'I don't want to talk about it.'

'If someone's been hassling you, you have to tell me.'

'I don't want to talk about it.'

'Spud –'

'Leave me alone.'

'Spud, I'm not going away. You'll have to tell me sooner or later. If I know what's going on, I can help you when it comes to dealing with Mum. She's pretty annoyed at being called to the school.'

'Nick off, Jess.'

'I'm just going to sit down right outside your door and sing Abba songs until you let me in.' Jess sat down and began. She sounded woeful.

The door opened a crack. She could just see Spud's eyes. They were swollen from crying. Puffy and red. He was about to shut the door again, but she jammed her foot in front of it just in time.

She pushed it open. Spud didn't resist.

'Oh my God, Spud! What happened to your neck?'

Spud's neck was covered in bruises. Green, yellow and purple. It looked like someone had grabbed him by the throat.

'I ran into a tree on my bike.'

'That's crap. What happened?'

Silence.

'Spud, did this happen because of me?' Jess's voice was unusually quiet. She fought back the tears. But she sounded croaky, which gave her away.

Spud just nodded.

'Because you kept my secret?'

Another nod.

Jess wasn't sure what to do. Weakly, she sat down on the bed beside Spud, and handed him a tissue to wipe the tears from his cheeks. They were flowing freely now. He cried. Hacking, wrenching sobs.

They sat for a long time. Jess tentatively put her arm around her brother. He didn't push her away.

Jess didn't know what to say. So she said, 'I'm sorry.' Then she said gently, 'I need to know what's been happening so that I can try to fix it. I'm so sorry that you've been hurt. I want to make sure that it never happens again. You're my favourite kid brother in the whole world. I'm so sorry.'

'It's OK. I mean, it's not OK but I know you couldn't help it.'

Spud's breathing was still interrupted now and again by convulsions from his sobbing. 'I was so scared, Jess. The other times I've managed to get away, but this time I couldn't.'

Spud's voice broke off. He sat up, blew his nose and looked his sister squarely in the face, as though he was about to say something. Then he looked away from her and stared at his big toe instead.

'Were you at school today, Spud?'

He shook his head. No.

'I just went to pick up my bike after school. It was late. There were still a few cars in the teachers' car park so I figured I was safe.'

'What happened to you?'

'I was getting a drink of water from the drinking taps, and then I got this feeling. All of a sudden, I just knew that he was there.'

'Who? Who was there, Spud?' Jess was trying hard

to hold it together, but she was becoming more frustrated. 'For heaven's sake, who are we talking about?'

Suddenly, Spud snapped. 'Your boyfriend's best friend, Mike.' Spud spat the name out angrily.

'Oh, Spud.' Jess had always considered Mike to be harmless.

Spud was on a roll. 'He's been following me for days, Jess. I've lost count of the times. At first I thought it was sort of funny cos he looked like he was playing dress-ups with his stupid clothes. Doofus Mike in his dickhead studded boots and girly jacket. And then he just turned up everywhere I went. He even managed to sneak into the school playground to find me when no one was watching. He got me, right outside the stupid toilets at recess. He was saying dumb things like, "No one stuffs around with my mate and gets away with it," and "Nothing will save you this time, Spud," and just being a complete loser.'

'Idiot. My God, he must have serious problems.' Jess couldn't believe what she was hearing.

'You don't say.' Spud swiped a fleck of spit off his arm. 'He's a sicko, Jess. He really gets a kick out of scaring kids that aren't as big as he is. And no one's got any chance of growing as big and boofy as him. Then he said he'd rip my head off and spit down my neck if I didn't tell him what he wanted to hear.

'Mike's even waited for me by the lockers. That's why I couldn't go to school, Jess. Cos you wouldn't tell your stupid boyfriend that you've got stupid cancer. Twice he nicked off just as he was about to get sprung. I tell ya, I just wish Mr Simpson had hurled his spotty bum into the office and made him pay.'

Spud paused for breath. Then, more quietly, he continued. 'And today he got me. In front of some other kids too. Idiot. That stinky-breath dickhead with his mangy ugly head and his chipped teeth had me up against the wall. And then he grabbed me round the neck. I could hardly breathe. I should have just spewed all over him, the loser. He is *such* a loser.'

Jess chose her words carefully. 'Why, Spud? I still don't understand exactly what he wanted, and what it has to do with me.'

'He wanted to know everything about you.'

'About me?'

'Where you've been hiding out and why you won't talk to Dylan. And he couldn't find you, could he? Cos you're all safe and snug at home with cancer. So he found me instead.'

'Spud, I can't believe it.'

'Yeah, well, you'd better believe it. The only reason I'm here now is that Dylan showed up.'

'Dylan? Did he see what was happening?'

'I don't know and I don't care, Jess. They're both total losers. You have no idea how hard it's been for me to keep your stupid secret. You know I always keep my promises. I haven't told one stupid person. And now I'm the one being punished for it. Nothing's like it used to be. Stupid secrets. Stupid dumb cancer.'

Jess was incredulous. 'Why didn't you tell me?'

'I don't know. I was too pissed off. You should have talked to Dylan ages ago. I told you that ages ago. You didn't listen then, so why would you listen now?'

'Did he hurt you badly?'

'I got away just before he did anything else. He let go of me when he heard Dylan coming. Gutless. I just ran and ran and ran. I didn't even pick up my bike. I hope it's still there. When I got home I heard you and Mum talking and I couldn't stop crying. I couldn't breathe properly either so I just opened the gate as quietly as I could and climbed the big tree. I waited there until Mum went out.'

'Then you came inside.'

'And listened to you singing crappy songs. And now you know everything.'

'Stupid dumb cancer.' They both said it at the same time.

Chapter 17

Decision Time

Jess and Spud sat on the bed in silence for a long time. Finally, Jess turned to Spud. 'I'll have to do something about this.'

Spud looked alarmed. 'What can you do? What if you get hurt as well?'

'I don't think that'll happen.' Jess reached over and gave Spud a hug. They both wiped the leftover tears from their eyes, and then the wire front door slammed. 'That's Mum. If you like, I'll tell her what's been going on.' Jess knew that it would be really hard for Spud to face their mother with this information. And that it would be hard for Ruby to hear it.

Spud nodded gratefully, wiping a big bogey from his nose with the back of his arm.

'Get a tissue, you grot,' said Jess as she ruffled his hair. 'I'll be back.'

And Jess headed off to the kitchen to fill Ruby in on the gory details. She also had an important phone call to make.

Chapter 18

Closing In

'Hi, is Dylan there please? It's Jess.'

Jess was frantically shooing her mother away, trying to get her to go back into the lounge room where she had been comfortably sitting with a magazine when Jess had dialled the number. Ruby always snuck in to listen to her phone calls. It was just one in a succession of frustrating things about having a mother.

'Yep. I can wait a minute . . . No, we haven't met . . . Jess McAllister . . . Yeah, that's right, Benfield High . . . Oh, OK. Do you expect him back soon? He's with Rosie . . . Oh, OK . . . Yep . . . Bye.'

Jess put down the receiver and sat down heavily on the stool. Dylan was out with Rosie. Her heart sank. She felt used and stupid and violated. If he already had another girlfriend, what was the big deal with Spud's being harassed and beaten up? Why didn't he just leave Spud alone? She could just picture them having a good old laugh at her expense. And gloating about how they'd got her little brother.

Everything made sense now, though. That was why he hadn't contacted her. He had someone else just waiting in the wings. He probably had a whole string of girls just dying to be with him. What an actor, too. Sara had been so convinced that he was really upset. Yeah, right. Poor Dylan was so upset that he went and got someone else straight away.

Now that she thought about it, Jess had never heard of a Rosie around Benfield High. Maybe she was at one of the other local schools. Or maybe she didn't go to school at all. Dylan was the sort of guy who would easily charm an older woman.

Jess picked up the phone and slammed it down again. Now what should she do? Dylan wouldn't ring her back. Not after being out with Rosie. What reason would he have to talk to stupid Jess again?

Damn it. Jess kicked the cupboard. Ruby raised an eyebrow and coughed to remind Jess that the earlier shooing hadn't worked. She was still there. And Jess had forgotten.

'What?' Jess looked angrily at her mother.

'I didn't say a thing,' said Ruby, lifting her hands in a submissive gesture.

No, thought Jess, but you don't have to say a thing out loud and I still know exactly what you're thinking, Mum. It comes through loud and clear.

'Good. Don't. I don't need to hear your opinions on this too. I'm sick of listening to your voice.'

'Jess, I don't think you should talk to me like that.'

'Mum, just shut up. I can't listen to you right now. Please, just shut up.' Jess ran to her room.

She lay on the bed for a little while, thinking. She wrapped the pillow round her head to cover her ears – to cocoon herself from the outside world. And after ten minutes she began to feel stronger.

Thank goodness she hadn't told him about her illness. Imagine how he would have reacted to knowing that. It was probably better in the long run. At least now she could see him for who he really was. And she would be able to get over her emptiness at breaking up with him much more quickly.

'Jess – '

'Go away, Mum.'

'I'd be delighted to remove myself from your rudeness and I will. Right now. I just thought you might like to know that there's a young man on the phone for you.'

Jess sat bolt upright. 'What's his name?'

'I believe it's Dylan.'

'Mum, would you please not hang around while I'm talking?'

'Very well. I'll do my breathing exercises. You should do yours too. Don't forget.'

Jess approached the telephone with great trepidation. Before, when she had called him, she had worked out exactly what she would say. Now, she felt like a blithering idiot.

It would probably be best just to get straight to the point. Get the whole thing over and done with. After all, Dylan probably had to get back to Rosie.

Jess cleared her throat. 'Hello, Dylan?'

There was a pause.

'Hi, Jess.'

'Hi.'

'Um, you called a moment ago. I didn't expect to hear from you.'

'No, I bet you didn't.'

'What?'

'Nothing.' Jess took a deep breath. It was now or never. 'I understand you've been seeing a bit of my little brother lately.'

'No. I don't really know your brother – oh yeah, hang on. I did see him – he was with Mike. Dunno why. That's right. I'd almost forgotten.'

'Too much else on your mind, probably.'

'Yeah, probably.'

But there was confusion in his voice. Like he wasn't sure what Jess was getting at. As if he didn't know.

'I wasn't, like, hanging out with your brother if that's what you mean.'

'No. That's not what I mean.' Jess was being a nasty cow but she couldn't stop herself.

'Oh.'

A silence.

'Jess, I don't know what you're on about. I didn't expect to hear from you ever again after that letter you sent me. With NO explanations. I wasn't supposed to contact you. I haven't even caught sight of you for weeks. And now, all of a sudden, you ring up with this really weird attitude like you hate me or I've done something awful to you and all I can think of is that I want you to say you're sorry.'

'Oh, yeah right, I'm sorry.'

'And that you made a mistake and you want to see me again.'

'What?' Jess couldn't believe her ears. 'I think you must have a screw loose somewhere, Dylan.'

Jess was about to hang up on him but remembered just in time why she wanted to talk to him. She put on the most sarcastic voice she could manage.

'Well, Dylan, if you have time between your social engagements with Rosie, perhaps you'd care to call your horrible friend off my little brother. Personally, I have no idea why you even hang out with him.'

Jess didn't even pause for breath before continuing. 'You know, Dylan, it's a really low act to go after someone's little brother, especially when they're as small as Spud is. But then, on top of that, to get someone else to do your dirty work for you is downright pathetic. Just pathetic.'

There was another silence. Then he said, 'Have you finished?'

'Not quite. I'm catching my breath.'

'Well, I can't listen to any more of this crap.'

'Fine.'

'Fine.'

Dylan hung up first. Jess couldn't believe it. How dare he. Jess slowly put the telephone receiver down. This wasn't how she had planned the conversation. She slumped on to the stool again. Ruby slid a glass of water down the bench to her. Funny, that. She was always around at the right time.

Jess took a sip of water. She couldn't make eye contact with her mother.

'You really like this boy, don't you, Jess?'

Jess just nodded.

'Maybe you need to talk to him properly,' said Ruby, kindly but firmly. 'Nothing ever gets sorted out when you're accusing someone. Of course Dylan was going to be defensive when you spoke to him like that.'

'Are you on his side?'

'I'm not on anyone's side. What you've told me about – is it Mike? – and what he did to Spud is terrible. He is a disturbed young man, and we'll take the appropriate measures to deal with it. Poor old Spud. As if he didn't already have enough to deal with.'

'I know. I just can't believe it.'

'But Jess, I think you're jumping to conclusions about Dylan. From what I can gather, it's quite possible that he didn't know.'

'This is just great. So you think I should ring him back.'

'Yes, I do.'

Good grief. Ruby had never said anything like this before. What was she on?

'I just think it's important for you to get to the bottom of this. You don't want any unfinished business with this boy. Just do it.'

Jess sighed. Her mother was probably right, but she certainly wasn't going to admit that to her. 'I'll think about it.'

'Good. You do that.' Ruby disappeared, leaving Jess with a glass of water, a rapid heartbeat and a clock ticking away very loudly on the kitchen wall.

Damn it. She dialled his number. And hung up immediately.

Again, she dialled. Slowly this time.

'Hello?' Dylan picked it up on the first ring.

'It's me again. Can I just say something please?' Jess's voice was wavering a bit.

'That depends on what you're going to say.'

'I'm not sure what I'm going to say. I just feel like we need to finish this conversation properly.'

Was Ruby inside her brain and controlling the words as they came out? Jess couldn't quite believe what she was saying. And even though she tried with all her might, she couldn't be mad at Dylan. This was ridiculous. The guy was probably arranging systematic beatings of her little brother and going out with someone else. She should just hate him. But she couldn't.

'Jess, most of what you've said makes no sense to me at all. Yes, I have been spending a lot of time with Rosie – '

Jess couldn't let him finish this sentence. 'You know what? I don't even care about that. And I don't want my nose rubbed in it either. What you do is your business. You're the one who has to live with yourself.'

'Rosie's not –'

'Dylan, I really don't want to talk about her.'

'But you need to know.'

'No, I don't,' Jess said. 'What I need to know is why you let Mike frighten Spud to within an inch of his life, and then beat him up? His neck is black and blue and he's so frightened that he won't even go to school.'

'What?' The surprise in his voice almost seemed genuine. He was a good actor, she'd grant him that.

'Oh, come on, Dylan. Be honest. Spud's in a terrible way and you let it happen.'

Dylan was silent.

'Dylan?'

More silence.

'Dylan?'

And then he spoke in a quiet voice. 'I can't believe you think that.'

'Why wouldn't I?'

'It's just – well, you obviously don't know me very well. I wouldn't sit back while someone else got hurt. Not if I could help, anyway.'

Jess gulped. Somehow, somewhere, she had known this all along. She desperately wanted to believe him.

'But Mike. Why would he just go and do something like that?'

'Mike's just Mike. I've stopped trying to figure him out. He must have thought he was doing me a favour.' Dylan sounded weary. 'I need to see you. I'll be there in ten minutes.'

Before she could answer, Dylan had hung up. That was that. He'd be here soon.

Jess would have to dig out the old woolly hat again.

Chapter 19

Spud's Revenge

Jess ran around the house trying to hide everything that might give her away.

The hats, the books on cancer that were on the coffee table, the medication, the sick buckets, the warm fluffy blankets, the meditation pyramid – Ruby's latest gizmo – were quickly relegated to hiding spots. Under the couch, behind the bookshelves.

A thought suddenly occurred to Jess. Spud! She'd need to tell him straight away that Dylan was coming over. She hoped it wouldn't traumatise him too much.

Strangely, Spud seemed very calm with the news that Dylan was coming to visit. In fact, he almost had a smile on his face.

The doorbell rang.

Oh shit, oh shit. Jess wasn't ready. She didn't know what to do. She ran and sat on the toilet. Ruby would answer the door.

Jess could hear Dylan's voice. He must be talking to Ruby, thought Jess. Funny that she couldn't hear her mother's voice, though. It usually resonated throughout the whole house.

Something was up. Dylan was talking way too loudly. In fact, he wasn't talking – he was yelling. Maybe he was just nervous about meeting Jess's mum. Anxiety could bring out strange behaviours in people. Bummer. Jess couldn't make out what he was saying.

And then Jess heard the back door slam. She immediately poked her head out of her hiding spot. There was Ruby, humming a tune, coming up the passage with the washing basket under her arm. She had been in the back yard all this time. So who was Dylan yelling at, at the front door?

No prizes for guessing.

Jess left the safety of the smallest room in the house and quickly crept toward the entrance hall.

There was Spud, with the safety latch firmly in

place, tormenting Dylan by pulling his fingers apart as hard as he could. Needless to say, only Dylan's hand was stuck inside the door – the rest of his body was safely outside and that was just how Spud wanted it.

'Spud!'

He turned to her. His face was a curious sight. Smugness, defiance and serenity, all at once. His eyes were so strange – like they were on fire. He didn't even seem to see Jess. He looked right through her.

Jess gulped. She had never seen her little kid brother so spooky. 'Spud, what are you doing?'

Spud didn't answer. He just stood silent, for what seemed like an eternity. Then he abruptly turned to the door and said, 'Bye, Dylan,' in a calm voice.

Jess relaxed a little. But just as she was breathing a sigh of relief, Spud spun on one foot and slammed the door on to Dylan's hand. Then he shot past Jess like a rocket. Spud was off out the back door. She had no hope of catching him. So she turned her attention to matters at hand. Dylan's hand, in fact.

It didn't look very good at all. When Jess opened the door, Dylan sort of fell into the hallway. His face was pale and he was sort of clammy to touch. Ruby had joined them, alerted by Spud's speedy exit to the fact that a drama was unfolding at the front of the house.

She immediately lunged into action. 'Come on, love, I'll get you some ice for that. It looks nasty.'

The three of them moved into the kitchen. It was fortunate that all the attention was on Dylan's hand. Fortunate for Jess, anyway. Her nerves had had some time to settle and had almost disappeared completely. And she and Dylan hadn't even spoken yet!

So it was that Jess found herself sitting on the cold bathroom floor with Dylan, holding his mangled hand under the bath tap (there was no ice in the freezer and the kitchen sink was full of dirty dishes), before they'd even said hello.

'I'll go and grab some ice from the service station. Keep that hand under the water, Dylan. Don't move until I get back.' Ruby left quickly.

Suddenly, Jess became self-conscious. She focused all her attention on Dylan's hand, even though she could feel that he was looking at her. He was willing her to look back at him. But to look at him right now would be the hardest thing in the world to do.

116

'Aren't you even going to say hello?'

'Hello.' She still hadn't lifted her head.

'Oh, hi. Glad we got that out of the way.'

Jess could feel a smile creeping its way on to her face. She allowed herself a sideways glance. That was it. No more holding back. She lit up in a big fat smile and Dylan did the same. They sat there for a second. It was sort of nice, sort of awkward and sort of weird.

'Well, it was good chatting with Spud,' Dylan offered. Jess broke into a giggle. Dylan laughed too.

'Ow, ow, ow.' He had moved his hand away from the stream of water.

'Put it back. You heard what Sister Ruby said.'

'Your mum seems nice,' said Dylan as he realigned his body into a different contortion so he could balance his arm on the edge of the bath and still look at Jess when they spoke.

'Yep. Good old Ruby. She really is a nurse, you know. She's been great looking after me when I have che – '

Damn. Jess had nearly given herself away. Maybe Dylan hadn't noticed her slip. She bit her lip and quickly changed the subject. She said, 'So, do you think anything's broken?'

'Yeah, I do actually. I wouldn't be surprised if I've cracked one of the smaller bones in my hand. I did it once before. It feels pretty similar.'

Jess did a double take. She hadn't expected him to answer with a yes. 'Oh, you poor thing. It must be really hurting.'

'Yeah, it is, but I'm OK. Have you got any painkillers?'

'Yep, up here. Keep your hand under the water.' Jess got up and opened the bathroom cupboard. A few boxes fell on to the floor. Both she and her mother were always cramming in new boxes without chucking away the old ones. They were mainly anti-nausea tablets for Jess. And stomach settlers, and super-strength painkillers.

Jess quickly picked up the boxes and shoved them back into the cupboard, not wanting Dylan to see them. She kept some painkillers aside.

'Do they work for you?' Dylan nodded at the pinkish packet that was lying near the basin.

Jess stopped wrestling with the tablet she was trying to release from its plastic bubble. She wasn't sure she'd heard him right.

'What?' she asked slowly.

She could feel a burning sensation make its way from her neck up into her cheeks.

'Do they work for you?'

'You mean these?'

'Yeah.' Dylan's eyes were studying one of the empty boxes on the floor. 'They're to stop the nausea, right?'

Jess was silent.

'You take one straight after your treatment.'

Jess thought that her head might explode. What was Dylan doing? Her face was so hot, she knew that she was a strong shade of beetroot. If only the floor would open up and swallow her.

Dylan wasn't about to let the subject rest. 'When you've had chemotherapy, they give you those drugs to stop the nausea.'

Jess felt like she would stop breathing right then and there. Her heart was racing. How did he know all this?

Time seemed to stand still.

Dylan continued, 'My mum had them.'

Jess looked up at him. 'I didn't know your mum had canc – was, was sick.' Where her voice came from, she didn't know.

119

'Yeah, well, she was. She was diagnosed with cancer eighteen months ago.'

Jess took a breath. 'You've never spoken about it.'

'Yeah, I know. It's a bit hard. Dad never wanted anyone to know, really. So I sort of kept it to myself.'

'Did your mum . . . ?'

'Yep. She died. Eleven months ago. It all happened in a blur after she was diagnosed.' He was talking too quickly, even for Dylan. Now it was his turn to avoid eye contact. Jess thought she saw his lip quiver. Jess didn't know what to do. The sound of the running water was suddenly very loud.

'How did you – ' Jess was struggling to string her words together. Everything else seemed insignificant.

'How did I know about you?'

'Well, yeah.'

'I just put two and two together, Jess. I didn't have to be a rocket scientist to figure it out. The clues were all there. They've been staring me in the face all along and I just didn't pick up on them.'

Jess was stunned. She couldn't think of anything to say. So she handed Dylan two painkillers and a glass of water.

'What sort of cancer is it?'

Jess couldn't look at him at all now. 'Lymphoma. It's a good one to get, if that makes sense. Like, they can treat it and half the time it just goes away.' Jess was trying to be nonchalant and act like it was nothing much.

It wasn't really working.

'So this is what you've been "dealing" with, like you said in the letter? And why you broke up with me?'

Jess couldn't speak any more. She felt both numb and raw, exposed, at the same time. She nodded.

'Jeez.' Dylan sighed. 'Why didn't you tell me?'

Jess's voice kind of came back, enough for her to say, 'I tried, I just . . . oh, I don't know.'

Dylan was quiet for some time. 'I would have understood, you know. I used to just feel sick all the time when Mum was sick. The secrets made me sick. It felt like part of me had cancer too. Not talking about it was stupid. It was Dad's idea not to talk about it. But why? In the end, she still died.'

'So you didn't talk about it at all?'

'Nah. Dad turned into a bit of a nutcase. We

didn't mention it, even when Mum was still alive.'

'That must have been so weird. In your house, I mean.'

'Not really. We just treated her like she was normal. It was weird after she died. Then I had to write lots of stuff.'

'What do you mean?'

'A journal. I just wrote things down when it all got too much at home. It's funny, a while ago I thought that I'd end up showing it to you some day.'

There was a silence.

'I didn't tell you because I didn't know if you'd understand or not.' Jess cast him a glance before studying the floor with some intensity.

Another silence. It was deafening.

'So, what's happening with you now? Are you OK?'

'I don't know. I'm still having chemo. Two more treatments to go. I'm getting really sick of it. In fact, I hate it. It sucks.'

Dylan nodded. 'It's pretty full-on. I saw what happened to Mum.' He absent-mindedly picked at the candle wax on the bath ledge. 'I'm just sad that you didn't tell me, Jess. All this time, I've been thinking . . . '

Dylan suddenly grimaced with pain. His hand was swelling rapidly and turning an interesting shade of blue.

'Keep it under the water. Mum'll be back soon.'

He composed himself. And changed the subject.

'So, is that the way Spud greets all your guests?'

'Mostly.'

Dylan raised an eyebrow.

'Oh, all right then, no. You got special treatment!'

'And, again, I wouldn't need to be a rocket scientist to figure out that Spud thinks I put Mike up to harassing him. So that's why he hates me.'

'Yep. I guess that's it, in a nutshell.'

'Do you think there's any point in talking to him now?'

'I don't think you'll find him. We don't see him for dust when he wants to get away, and he sure wanted to get away from you!'

Dylan nodded. 'Mike's really lost it. I don't suppose there's much point in saying sorry?'

'Not really.'

'No.'

A silence.

'Sorry, anyway.'

At that moment, Ruby arrived home with some ice. She inspected Dylan's hand and wrapped some ice in a tea towel to cool it. 'OK, love. I think you might have a little break here. We'll need to get you to the hospital for an x-ray.'

Ruby turned to Jess with her back to Dylan. She mouthed the words, 'Did Spud do this?'

Jess nodded at her mother. Ruby rolled her eyes heavenwards. Out loud she said, 'Sometimes I don't know what gets into Spud. I have no idea of the way that his little mind works.'

Jess held the door open for them as Ruby led the way to the car.

'I'm going to call you,' Dylan said as he was bundled past her.

Jess smiled. 'I hope your hand's OK.'

'Thanks.'

'Jess, I don't want you coming out now. It's too cold. Get back into the warm and think about putting some rice on for dinner. I'll go to the hospital with Dylan and make sure that his family know he's there.'

And then they were gone. Dylan and Jess's mother.

What a combination.

Good grief!

Chapter 20

No Escape

Yippee! Jess celebrated as she slurped on a chocolate thickshake and sauntered through the shopping centre with Sara.

They had half an hour to roam about and do as they pleased before meeting up with Sara's mum in front of Coles.

Jess felt like she'd been let out of a cage. And it was so nice to be away from Ruby. She was just doing her job and being a mother – albeit an overprotective mother – but Jess felt like she had been granted a pardon or a reprieve because she was out and about.

She didn't even care that it was Friday afternoon and loads of local schoolkids would be hanging out in the shopping centre. Didn't care that she would walk past groups of kids who all knew she was sick and might whisper. Didn't care that she looked different and often had to lean on nearby seats (she wasn't *so* sick that she had to sit on them) and even once on Sara when she ran out of energy for a moment.

This was living! How easy it was to forget that there was a whole world out there. Jess knew that hiding the truth from Dylan had not been good for her, either physically or emotionally, but she seriously felt like she had been born again. It was like she was just gliding around on thin air.

The way she felt now, she could deal with anything. Even stupid old cancer!

'What do you think of these, Jess?' Sara had on a pair of trainers with chunky heels.

'I think you should go for a test jog around the store,' said Jess as she sucked loudly on the dregs of her milkshake.

The saleswoman looked up at them over the tip of her horn-rimmed glasses. She was almost straight out of a clichéd novel. The type of shop owner who would keep her beady eyes on every young person

127

who came into her shop in case they stole something.

Sara shook the shoes off her feet. 'I'd never make the volleyball team in these.' And to the woman: 'Thank you so much for your time.'

The shop assistant did a bit of a double-take at Sara's politeness. Sara could be a real brown-noser when she wanted to. But as her mother often said, it costs nothing to be nice to people even if they are giving you the evil eye.

'I need a greasy potato cake and a dim sim,' said Sara as they came out of the shoe shop. They started to make their way down to the café that was away from where all the local kids hung out. Neither of them said, 'Let's not go to the usual place,' they just both headed for the quieter option.

'Hey, Jess, isn't that Dylan?'

Jess's heart skipped a beat. It was only yesterday that he'd been at her place. A big part of her wanted to run up and say hi and tuck him under her arm and whisk him off into the sunset. Unfortunately, the other part wanted to hide under a rock for twenty years. So she just said, 'Where?'

'Straight ahead. Sitting with the girl in the blue jumper. Long hair.'

Rosie! thought Jess immediately. That must be Rosie. Since yesterday, she'd had all these romantic notions that she might have been wrong about Dylan – that Rosie didn't exist and Jess was the one that Dylan wanted to be with. But here it was, plain as the nose on her face and the woolly hat on her head. She could see with her own eyes that it wasn't to be.

Damn. He'd seen them. But he didn't smile. He probably didn't even want to talk to Jess after what Spud did. Jess's feet were suddenly dead weights. She had to consciously drag them every step as they moved closer to the café.

'Come on,' whispered Sara as she linked arms with Jess. 'Cheer up. We don't have to stay if you don't want to. Let's just say "hi" and see what's going on.'

Jess squeezed her elbow. She knew she was lucky to have a friend like Sara.

'OK,' she said without too much conviction. 'Here goes.'

And so they casually walked toward the table where Dylan and Rosie were sitting, having what seemed to be an engrossing conversation. Dylan was now very animated, smiling loads and making goo-goo eyes.

'Look at the faces he's pulling. He's blowing kisses and stuff. Sara, I can't do this.'

'Come on.' Sara wasn't about to stop now.

'Look at her. Even her stupid hair's gorgeous!'

'Just keep your cool. Don't worry.'

As they approached the table Dylan jumped out of his seat and came over to them.

'Hi. It's great to see you.' He fixed Jess with that penetrating stare that turned her legs to jelly.

'Hi.' Jess smiled and did a little accidental dance on the spot as she tried not to fall over.

'It's good to see you too, stranger,' said Sara, punching him in the shoulder. 'Jess told me what happened to your hand. Give us a look.'

Dylan held out a bandaged hand. He seemed kind of embarrassed but he was smiling a bit too.

'Oh my God. What a crack-up!' Sara laughed too loudly at her own joke.

'Yeah, right.' Dylan gave Sara a return friendly punch in the arm.

'Mum told me that it wasn't broken. She said that it was just a really bad bruising.' Jess was intently inspecting the bandage around Dylan's hand. She couldn't look him in the eye.

'It's gonna be fine. I bet Spud was disappointed.'

'I'd like to say no but I think he was. He's not going to let you off easily. It was your mate who beat him up.'

'Yeah, I know.' Dylan was beginning to look uncomfortable now. He shoved his hands – bandage and all – deeply into his pockets and shifted his weight from one foot to the other.

'My old man's taking Mike to see a social worker today. He's messed up pretty bad. In his head, I mean.'

For a moment, no one said anything.

'I guess there's a lot to be forgiven.' Dylan looked up at Jess.

'Yeah. I guess there is.'

Sara seized the awkward moment and gestured in Rosie's direction. 'So, are you going to introduce us?'

Jess kicked Sara lightly in the shin but Dylan didn't notice. He was very preoccupied.

For a moment, he looked confused, like he'd almost forgotten she was even there!

'Oh, yeah. Of course.'

Jess hadn't been game to look at her, like, really look at her, until now. She didn't want to seem like she was staring or anything.

'Um . . . Jess, Sara, this is Rosie,' said Dylan as they came to the table. Jess was glad there was a seat right there for her to sink into. The girl was bouncing a baby on her knee. 'And this is Teresa.' The girl with long hair smiled. 'She looks after Rosie when me and Dad can't.'

'Hi,' said Teresa and smiled warmly. Rosie just gurgled and chucked up her banana smoothie.

'Uh oh, I've been smoothied again,' said Teresa, with a grimace.

'Glad I'm not holding her,' said Sara as she flashed Jess a conspiratorial smile and kicked her shins lightly as a payback. So, Dylan didn't have a girlfriend called Rosie at all! But he'd never mentioned a baby.

'Dylan, I'll have to be getting back to the centre. Everything seems to be OK now.'

'Yep. Thanks for your help. She wasn't going to come home without having a smoothie with you.'

'I love it. And don't you dare tell any of the other parents, but Rosie's my favourite.'

Rosie cooed at Teresa and gave her a big sloppy kiss. Teresa didn't seem to mind at all. Jess and Sara both recoiled a little bit. Kisses with banana bits were not their idea of a good time.

'Bye, then. I'll see you Thursday. Nice to meet you, Jess and Sara.'

'Yeah, you too.' Teresa smiled and left.

Rosie burped and dribbled some more. Dylan threw her on to his right shoulder which was covered with a cloth nappy. He was obviously an old hand at this.

'I told you I had something to tell you about Rosie,' he said with a little grin.

'Is she – ?' Sara began.

'She's my sister.'

Jess nodded, trying to look composed and interested and not in the least surprised. She said nothing.

Sara spoke for both of them. 'You never told us that you had a sister.'

'She was only six months old when Mum died. She was a mid-life surprise for my folks. So we've had to look after her the best we can. Dad and I.'

'Dylan, I – we had no idea,' Sara started to say.

133

'It doesn't matter. What usually happens is that we can arrange it so one of us is home to look after her, but lately it's all been stuffed up. Dad was sick and I was just really weird.' He stopped and didn't look directly at Jess, but all three of them knew what he was talking about.

'How old is she?' asked Jess.

'Seventeen months. Sometimes it feels like she's five or something, you know. She knows stuff that you wouldn't believe. It can be a real spin-out.'

It was all making sense. So this was why Dylan had left school without any explanation. To look after his sister while his dad worked.

Rosie started to bang on the table with her spoon, and then she hit Dylan on the head with it. She laughed as he made 'this is hurting me' type faces. But she didn't stop, she just giggled a lot. And Dylan didn't take the spoon away. Then she flicked little bits of banana smoothie all over Sara. Jess snorted with laughter. Rosie gurgled with delight. Sara managed a little smile before picking the remnants of banana off with a very goopy look on her face.

Dylan handed her a serviette. 'It goes with the territory. Dribble and nappies.'

Sara glanced at her watch. 'Oh my God. Mum! We were supposed to meet her ten minutes ago.'

'OK. Well, I guess we'd better go. It was really nice running into you, Dylan,' smiled Jess as she tried to prise her finger out of Rosie's grasp. For a baby, she sure had a strong grip.

'I'm glad you both met Rosie. Hey, see you around.'

As they turned to leave, Dylan pulled something out of his back pocket. It was a little dog-eared book with the front cover just about hanging off. He pressed it into Jess's hand. 'I was sort of hoping we'd bump into each other. I thought you might be interested in this.'

'Thanks.' It was Dylan's journal. Jess didn't know what to say. She was overcome. This was huge. He trusted her enough to show her his journal! 'I'll look after it for you.'

Dylan nodded and half looked at the ground. 'I know.'

As they wandered off, Jess could hear Rosie squealing behind them. She turned. Rosie was gleefully pulling Dylan's jumper up over his head. She waved. All of a sudden Jess felt blissfully happy.

'I told you there was nothing to worry about,' said Jess as she gave Sara a playful punch in the arm. There was a skip in her step as they walked through the shopping centre.

'You are so full of it,' smiled Sara. 'There's Mum.'

Chapter 21

Five Down, One to Go

Jess pinched herself. Ouch! Well, she definitely wasn't dreaming and she had the mark on her arm to prove it.

It was Charlotte! Right there, at the foot of her bed. Pigs might be known to fly after all! Jess had been laid up for three days since her last treatment. She had only one more to go – yippee!

When her mum had said that someone was here to visit, Charlotte was the last person Jess expected.

She looked thinner, and a bit pale. Sort of tired. There was something about her that was different. She seemed less confident in the way she was standing.

Jess wasn't sure what to do. Should she say, 'Hi, Charlotte. It's nice of you to finally drop by to check out whether I'm dead or not. Want a Mintie?'

It didn't feel quite right.

Charlotte looked like she wanted to say something anyway. She sat heavily on Jess's bed and held out the bunch of daffodils that she'd been gripping tightly.

'I didn't know what to bring you, so I just got some of these. They're like a symbol for people with cancer or something I think.' Charlotte looked away from Jess's gaze.

Jess said thank you. Charlotte almost seemed like a different person. Something was really bugging her.

'What's happening, Charlotte? What's going on?' Jess didn't have a lot of energy so she just cut to the important questions. 'What's taken you so long to come and visit, you noof?'

To her surprise, Charlotte started to cry.

'Charlotte, I didn't really mean you're a noof, I just thought it might make you more comfortable – '

'Damn, damn. I promised myself I wouldn't do this. All the way here, I'm thinking, Right – I'll just say what I need to say and leave it with you, and now here I am, blubbering like an idiot.'

Jess silently passed the tissue box. Charlotte took

a handful. She wiped her nose and then mopped up the river of mascara that was running down her face. It left streaks. She looked like Ozzy Osbourne, but Jess didn't say that to her.

Charlotte continued. 'The thing is, Jess, I've just never been good at hanging around sick people, you know? And Joffa's had all this stuff to do . . .' Her voice trailed off.

Jess was giving her a look. A sideways, one eyebrow up in the air look. One that said I know you're lying but I'm not going to say anything because I know you know too so just stop.

'OK, OK. I'll stop making excuses. But you have to stop looking at me like that.'

Jess's face softened.

'Fine. You want the truth? Here it is. First of all, I'm sorry. I can't hang around people who are sick. I nearly threw up myself coming in here to see you. But I'll spare you the Technicolor details.'

'Thanks,' Jess said sarcastically, but with a smile. She had missed Charlotte's straightforward way of talking.

There was the sound of a phone ringing. Charlotte lunged into her bag like a woman possessed and turned it off. She didn't even look at the number to see who was calling. This must be serious, thought Jess. It was.

'Second thing is, I'm pregnant. Four months pregnant, in fact. I only found out a few weeks ago. For God's sake close your mouth before you swallow a fly or something. You got cancer. I got pregnant. What's the big deal?'

Jess suddenly felt hot. She swallowed. 'Joffa's?'

For a moment, Charlotte seemed genuinely offended. But she got over it.

'Of course it's Joffa's, you noof. So . . . I've left school. But you probably know that already. Sara's done everything but take out a full page ad in the paper. I was expelled. Smoking. You know how it is.'

Jess didn't know how it was but that didn't matter.

'I haven't told many people about the baby. Dad nearly killed me when he found out, but he's come around to the idea. He can't say anything, anyway. Mum was only seventeen when I was born.'

Jess didn't say anything about Charlotte being sixteen. She didn't have to. Charlotte went on. 'So, we're going to get married next month and rent a bit further out of town. There's a house for lease on

Barn's Hill and Joffa's got some work out there.'

Charlotte paused for a breath. Jess was speechless.

'I don't know why I'm here telling you this. I've been a crap friend. I haven't been there at all for you. And I dunno why, I just had to come and tell you what's going on.'

She started to cry again. Jess had never seen Charlotte cry before. Not once in their twelve years of friendship. What should she say? What should she do? She felt totally helpless and, horribly, almost wished that Charlotte hadn't come to see her.

'Oh, man. I've got to stop this.' Charlotte sat up and blew her nose loudly. 'How's everything going for you, anyway?'

'Fine, good. OK. I'm still here.'

'Yeah. That's one good thing. You're still here.' A flicker of tenderness crossed Charlotte's face. Just for a moment. Then she said, 'Listen, I've got to go. Joffa's outside waiting and I – I've gotta go.' She was picking up her things and almost stumbling to get out of there as quickly as she could.

'Good luck with everything,' called Jess.

'Thanks. Um, you too.' Charlotte gave Jess an awkward hug, sort of slapped her on the back and made a beeline for the door. She couldn't get out of there quickly enough.

The engine roared as they drove off into the great unknown. Charlotte, Joffa and their baby. Jess watched them through the window. Watched until the car was a tiny speck in the traffic.

How their lives had changed. Were changing still.

Chapter 22

Go, Sara!

'And here's our book review assignment for next week.'

Sara handed it over with great aplomb. Jess glanced at it then tossed it back. No point getting all worked up about assignments that she couldn't do.

'You know, Jess. I think you were going a bit far when you decided to take the easy way out and have chemotherapy rather than stand up in front of the whole entire class to deliver your book report.'

'How did you go with your book report – it was today, wasn't it?'

'Oh, it went OK.' Sara looked totally smug and was being too non-committal for her own good. Jess just knew that something was up.

'You got an "A"? You always get an "A".'

Sara nodded.

Jess smiled. 'Good on you. And I bet Simon was impressed.' Jess knew that Sara must be in love with Simon because she'd mentioned him three times yesterday afternoon. For Sara, that was a record.

Sara blushed.

'Oh my God, you're blushing. Did you talk to him, or flick your hair in his direction, like a movie star?'

'Maybe.'

'You did, didn't you? See what happens when I'm not around to keep my eye on you.'

'Here.' Deftly, Sara chucked something fuzzy and colourful at Jess.

No, it wasn't a specialty toilet brush or a tie-dyed skunk. Jess couldn't guess any more so she opened the expensive plastic supermarket bag wrapping. It was a clown wig!

'Cool!' said Jess as she put it on. 'How did you know? It's just what I've always wanted. Now I can walk the streets of Benfield and not be recognised.'

'You don't have to thank me. The look on your face is gratitude enough,' said Sara sarcastically. 'By the way, I ran into Dylan this afternoon on the way here.' Sara paused for effect. It worked.

'And?' Jess could strangle Sara sometimes with her stupid dramatic pauses.

'He wants to come over with me on Friday to visit. He'll bring the pizza, I'll get the video. Only I won't be able to stay too long cos I've got to work at Mum's stall from seven. So you'll have to cope without me for the rest of the evening.'

'Is he bringing Rosie?'

'Nope. His dad's looking after her.'

'Oh. Well, I think I can work that into my busy schedule.'

'Your schedule? You've been watching too many bad daytime soaps. You need to get out more.'

'OK, OK. I'm sick of me, let's get back to you. So what exactly happened with Simon?'

'Well – nothing much, really.'

'Right. And I'm Kylie with no hair. What happened today?'

'Oh . . .' Sara was being way too calm and collected. And then she couldn't contain it any longer. 'I finally got up the courage to speak to him. And then, *he* asked *me* out! For tomorrow night!'

'Yippee!'

Both girls did a little jump up and down and hug one another dance.

'So are you going?' A superfluous question if ever there was one.

'Of course I'm going, you doofus. What do you think I am – crazy?'

They both cackled like hens. It was great to see Sara so happy and excited.

It was nice to feel genuinely happy.

She gave her friend a hug. For the third time that week, Jess forgot that she had cancer.

Chapter 23

The
Last One

Jess sat on the park bench with her mother, watching Spud perform his latest skateboard tricks.

He was getting really good at it, as he frequently liked to point out to her. He had been loads happier since the front door incident, and it seemed like he had almost forgiven Dylan. He had his bike back, he was going to school and he was even jumping on Jess's bed again. Things were definitely looking up for him.

And it had helped him to hear that Mike wasn't getting away with anything.

Apparently, Mike had been put on to some sort of good behaviour bond and had to spend time with a social worker. He was also made to help out with Dylan's dad at the garage for thirteen hours a week. Spud thought that it seemed like more of a punishment for Dylan's dad than anything else. But it did sort of balance things out a bit.

Spud had started to really annoy Jess again, which was a sure sign that things were getting back to normal.

Jess had just had her last treatment and felt like crap. But a million dollars worth of crap. It was great to know that this might be the end of it. She might never have to sit in that hospital day treatment room again. Fingers crossed.

She took a swig of water to flush the chemo through her system, and leaned into her mother's warm side. The wind was blowing a gale and Jess shivered. At least she knew she was alive.

'We'd better get you home soon,' said Ruby as she gave her daughter a squeeze.

'Ouch!' No matter how caring and gentle Ruby was in most ways, she always seemed to give Jess the biggest bear hugs in the world.

'Are you sure you feel up to going out tonight? You won't be able to eat anything, Jess. Why not wait and we'll celebrate properly when you're feeling better?'

Jess nodded. There would be time to celebrate the end of chemo when she felt up to it.

'And besides,' said her mum with a smile, 'Spud has sworn that he will not go to any restaurant with you wearing that ridiculous coloured wig.'

'Do you mean he doesn't like it?' Jess pretended to be surprised.

'That's right.'

Cool! Jess smiled, leaned back and closed her eyes. Now she had another piece of ammunition.

She was due to go back and see the specialist next week, to have an x-ray and blood test. They said she had to keep seeing the doctor for five years. After that, if the cancer had stayed away, she would be officially in remission. Jess sighed. It would be awesome to be declared 'In Remission', whatever that meant in the long term. She'd hate to have gone through all of this for nothing.

Although, it wasn't exactly for nothing. If she hadn't gone through all of this, Dylan might never have given her his journal to read. Funny how fate works. It was sort of like the cancer had given them permission to say things that they wouldn't have otherwise. Which was totally dumb when you thought about it.

Jess was glad that she had spoken about her feelings with Dylan. And that they'd spoken about Dylan's mum. And Dylan himself. And just about everyone else. Pretty stupid that she had to get cancer to realise it was OK to talk and share stuff.

And Rosie – she was just a crack-up. Jess was becoming really fond of her, but she still couldn't bring herself to change a dirty nappy. Especially a whiffy one.

She and Dylan had gone out a few days ago and an old lady had thought that Jess was Rosie's mum! Seriously! And Jess had sort of liked it, although she was way too young to have kids. She didn't even know if she'd be able to after all the chemo she'd had.

Charlotte had spoken to Sara. Apparently, she and Joffa got the house they'd been looking at, and everything was going fine. It was funny, Jess kind of knew that she wouldn't hear from Charlotte again, and she didn't mind. Things were different now. She would probably send her a little pair of booties or something when the baby was born.

And things were looking good with Dylan. They were taking it one day at a time now. Jess felt like she knew him heaps better since reading his journal. And since kissing him lots more! Bits of the journal had been sad and hard to read, but it was also inspiring to know that he had gone through times when he'd felt completely isolated from everyone else, and had come through to the other side. He was a pretty amazing person.

Jess still felt really alone lots of the time too. She was beginning to get the hang of talking about stuff, and there was a strange sense of comfort in knowing that she wasn't the only one to feel this way. Ruby was bringing home some brochures today about a cancer support group for teenagers. Jess felt up to giving it a try. It might even be good – she and Dylan could go there together.

Jess was beginning to choose healthy foods to eat even when her mother wasn't around, and she was feeling a lot more peaceful in herself, too. She was even learning to enjoy stir-fried brussels sprouts.

And lately, she'd been getting better at saying

what she was feeling. Even if other people didn't like it.

She still cried a lot. By herself, mostly. An iridologist had told her that crying is good for clearing out the lymphatic system – which was where she had cancer – so she was taking that literally. Watching really sad movies and really funny movies. But not at the same time!

Things were getting better at home, but they still weren't perfect. Her mum still bugged her sometimes, and often people acted like she needed to be wrapped in cotton wool. Occasionally she just wanted the ground to open up and swallow her.

Mostly, though, Jess was holding it together. Life still had moments of joy in between all the hard bits. She would have to repeat year eleven next year, but in a funny way, that was the least of her worries now. Sara would still be there doing year twelve, and anyway, she'd make new friends.

Jess pulled the clown wig out of her bag and put it on, over the top of her woolly hat. She whistled at Spud, who was doing a three-sixty on his skateboard.

He looked over.

'Spud!' Jess blew a kiss at him.

Spud shook his head in disgust. Then he grinned at her.

Jess smiled.

You only live once, she thought.

Unless you don't.

If you would like more information about
books available from Piccadilly Press and how
to order them, please contact us at:

Piccadilly Press Ltd.
5 Castle Road
London
NW1 8PR

Tel: 020 7267 4492
Fax: 020 7267 4493

Feel free to visit our website at
www.piccadillypress.co.uk